序　言

　　近年來，「大學入學學科能力測驗」及「指定科目考試」增加了「翻譯題」，題型是直接給兩題中文句子，請考生翻譯成英文。

　　現在，「大考中心」最新公佈的「學科能力測驗參考試卷」中，「翻譯題」出現了新題型。新題型是給一篇英文短文，裡面會有幾個地方以中文呈現，考生需利用上下文的線索，翻成英文。此種題型，在89年的「大學聯考」和85年的「學科能力測驗」都曾經出現過。

　　新的翻譯題型，不只考翻譯，也考閱讀，同學必須先讀完英文的文章，才能接著翻譯，且有時考的是「子句」，而非完整的句子，所以答題時須參考前後文的時態、句子結構，並考慮大小寫及標點符號的問題。

　　本書取材自各高中月期考試題，共有一百回測驗。每一回測驗，都有附上同學所寫的答案，我們再從中指出同學寫錯的地方，並加以改正。那些錯誤的地方，可能也是你會犯的錯誤。**我們改正後，再提供其他可能的答案**，同學不只可學到各種翻法，還可把所學的運用到英文寫作上，讓寫作能有多一點的變化。同學讀了此書，不僅在學校月期考中可得到高分，也同時準備了新的「學測」翻譯題型，一舉兩得。

　　本書雖經審慎校閱，疏漏之處，恐在所難免，誠盼各界先進不吝指正。

編者　謹識

本書答案範例由下列「劉毅英文」同學提供，謹此致謝。

姓 名	學 校	姓 名	學 校	姓 名	學 校
張博雄	板橋高中	謝家惠	大同高中	龔哲儀	北一女中
蘇郁雯	中山女中	郭彥汝	中山女中	陳柏玉	北一女中
杜長恩	三民高中	吳芳育	建國中學	蔡定璋	建國中學
林瑞怡	大直高中	孟耿德	中正高中	許登揚	建國中學
曹家豪	和平高中	郭子模	內湖高中	邱懷瑩	師大附中
黃孺雅	北一女中	江欣璇	北一女中	李冠瑢	薇閣高中
董巧儀	永春高中	黃楷婷	延平高中	張育維	延平高中
馬 筠	陽明高中	黃韻儒	北一女中	黃信和	成淵高中
曹如謹	北一女中	顏佑安	內湖高中	李佳顯	成功高中
李律恩	北一女中	殷偉珊	景美女中	董怡萱	中山女中
周芳睿	建國中學	陳政葦	建國中學	王劭予	建國中學
盧胤諮	中山女中	陳映儒	南湖高中	劉冠麟	師大附中
黃上瑋	建國中學	曹育彰	建國中學	李家萱	景美女中
林品君	景美女中	賴華沂	景美女中	陳柏君	建國中學
黃工哲	中正高中	陳麒琛	和平高中	張惟筑	中正高中
鍾秉軒	建國中學	李苡萱	北一女中	楊佳穎	中山女中
劉承疆	建國中學	黃致文	萬芳高中	謝采芸	成淵高中
劉娟安	板橋高中	于恩庭	北一女中	彭紀蕘	永平高中
葉家亨	延平高中	鄭筱彤	陽明高中	呂政哲	中正高中
邱煒翔	師大附中	梁 翔	西松高中	張若芃	中山女中
張淳富	建國中學	鄭 維	建國中學	林芳君	北一女中
張庭瑄	中山女中	陳彥廷	建國中學	游智勝	師大附中
張靜婷	西松高中	林浩存	建國中學	楊鈺涵	景美女中
林貝瑄	北一女中	劉 璇	中正高中	呂友文	成功高中
郭潤宗	師大附中	康 育	延平高中	林柔言	北一女中
張 涵	新店高中	傅子耘	北一女中	王瓊蕙	北一女中
蔡明倫	復興高中	陳品臣	建國中學	王家逸	延平高中
鄭文淇	師大附中	張維哲	華僑高中		
張晴茹	景美女中	陳樺彬	大同高中		

TEST 1

說明：下面一段短文中，有數處係以中文呈現，請利用上下
文線索（如單字、片語等）將其譯成正確、通順、達
意且前後連貫的英文。

Some types of body language, such as smiling when one is happy and tensing one's lips when one is angry, seem to be the same all over the world. Others, however, are not universal. They vary from one culture to another, and 1. 它們可能會造成人與人之間的許多誤會。 For example, in Japan, when parting with a friend, it is customary to give a bow, while in France, it is common to kiss a person on both cheeks. In any culture, the role of nonverbal messages cannot be underestimated. 2. 如果沒有它們，或許我們就幾乎完全無法溝通。 Therefore, when we learn another language, we must learn spoken language and body language alike.

1. ....

2. ....

TEST 1 詳解

1. *it may cause many misunderstandings between people.* 【誤】

（新店高中　張涵同學）

＊it 須改為 they，misunderstanding〔͵mɪsʌndə'stændɪŋ〕n. 誤會；誤解
為可數名詞，也可作不可數名詞。

$$
→ \text{they may}
\begin{cases}
\text{cause} \\
\text{lead to} \\
\text{give rise to} \\
\text{bring about} \\
\text{result in}
\end{cases}
\begin{cases}
\text{many misunderstandings} \\
\text{much misunderstanding}
\end{cases}
$$

$$
\begin{cases}
\text{among} \\
\text{between}
\end{cases}
\text{people.}
$$
【正】

2. *Without them, maybe we nearly can't communicate with each other.* 【誤】（新店高中　張涵同學）

＊「幾乎不能」須用 can hardly 表示，又依句意，為「與現在事實相反」
的假設，故用 could hardly。

$$
→
\begin{cases}
\text{But for them,} \\
\text{Without them,} \\
\text{If it were not for them,} \\
\text{Were it not for them,}
\end{cases}
\begin{cases}
\text{perhaps} \\
\text{maybe}
\end{cases}
\text{we could}
$$

　　hardly communicate at all. 【正】

【註釋】　tense〔tɛns〕v. 使拉緊　　lips〔lɪps〕n. pl. 嘴唇
　　　　　universal〔͵junə'vɝsḷ〕adj. 普遍性的
　　　　　vary〔'vɛrɪ〕v. 不同（= differ）　　part〔pɑrt〕v. 分開
　　　　　customary〔'kʌstəm͵ɛrɪ〕adj. 習慣性的；慣例的
　　　　　bow〔baʊ〕n. 鞠躬　　cheek〔tʃik〕n. 臉頰
　　　　　nonverbal〔nɑn'vɝbḷ〕adj. 非言辭的
　　　　　underestimate〔'ʌndɚ'ɛstə͵met〕v. 低估
　　　　　alike〔ə'laɪk〕adv. 同樣地

TEST 2

> 說明：下面一段短文中，有數處係以中文呈現，請利用上下
> 文線索（如單字、片語等）將其譯成正確、通順、達
> 意且前後連貫的英文。

A man may have many or few close friends in his life. A man may not really need many friends, but he needs some friends who can help and encourage him.

There are friends and friends. A good friend is much better than a fortune. 1. 他可以促進你的心智發展、激勵你，並且提升你的人格。 There is an old saying, "A man is known by the company he keeps." Tell me what company you keep, and I'll tell what you are, 2. 所以，選擇朋友時，你應該要非常小心。

1. ....

2. ....

TEST 2 詳解

1. _He can improve your mental development, inspire you, and enhance your characteristic._【誤】（建國中學 陳品臣同學）

   * enhance 是「加強」，應改為 uplift（提升）；characteristic（特性）應改為 character（人格）。

   → He $\left\{ \begin{array}{l} \text{can} \\ \text{is able to} \end{array} \right\}$ promote your $\left\{ \begin{array}{l} \text{mental} \\ \text{intellectual} \end{array} \right\}$

   $\left\{ \begin{array}{l} \text{development,} \\ \text{growth,} \end{array} \right\}$ $\left\{ \begin{array}{l} \text{inspire} \\ \text{motivate} \\ \text{encourage} \end{array} \right\}$ you, and $\left\{ \begin{array}{l} \text{uplift} \\ \text{improve} \end{array} \right\}$

   your $\left\{ \begin{array}{l} \text{character.} \\ \text{personality.} \end{array} \right\}$ 【正】

2. _therefore, you should be careful when you choose friends._【誤】

   （建國中學 陳品臣同學）

   *「非常」小心，所以 careful 前須加副詞 very。

   → so you $\left\{ \begin{array}{l} \text{should} \\ \text{ought to} \end{array} \right\}$ be $\left\{ \begin{array}{l} \text{very} \\ \text{extremely} \end{array} \right\}$ $\left\{ \begin{array}{l} \text{careful} \\ \text{cautious} \end{array} \right\}$

   $\left\{ \begin{array}{l} \text{in} \\ \text{when} \end{array} \right\}$ $\left\{ \begin{array}{l} \text{choosing} \\ \text{selecting} \end{array} \right\}$ friends. 【正】

【註釋】 close〔klos〕_adj._ 親密的
　　　　fortune〔'fɔrtʃən〕_n._ 財富；一大筆錢　　saying〔'seɪŋ〕_n._ 諺語
　　　　company〔'kʌmpənɪ〕_n._ 同伴；朋友　　keep〔kip〕_v._ 結交
　　　　**A man is known by the company he keeps.**【諺】觀其友，知其人。
　　　　**what** _sb._ _**is**_ 某人的人格　　promote〔prə'mot〕_v._ 促進
　　　　inspire〔ɪn'spaɪr〕_v._ 激勵　　motivate〔'motə,vet〕_v._ 激勵
　　　　uplift〔ʌp'lɪft〕_v._ 提升　　character〔'kærɪktɚ〕_n._ 人格
　　　　personality〔,pɜsn̩'ælətɪ〕_n._ 人格

TEST 3

> 說明：下面一段短文中，有數處係以中文呈現，請利用上下
> 文線索（如單字、片語等）將其譯成正確、通順、達
> 意且前後連貫的英文。

Newspapers are of great value. 1. 藉由看報紙，可以和全世界保持連繫。 The Chinese proverb says, "A scholar who stays at home can tell what is going on in the world." This is quite true. Newspapers tell us what is happening not only in our own country but also all over the world. 2. 編輯的意見，在大部分情況中，都能真實表達大眾的想法。 In fact, good newspapers are the mouthpiece of the nation and the unseen teachers of the common people.

1. ....

2. ....

TEST 3 詳解

1. <u>*By reading newspapers, we can keep in touch with all world.*</u>【誤】

（建國中學 陳彥廷同學）

* all world 須改為 all the world 或 the whole world，表「全世界」。

$$→ \begin{cases} \text{By reading a newspaper, one can} \\ \text{Reading a newspaper enables us to} \end{cases} \text{keep in touch}$$

with the whole world. 【正】

2. <u>*Editors opinions can convey public thoughts truely in many situations.*</u>【誤】（建國中學 陳彥廷同學）

* Editors 須改為所有格 Editors'；副詞 truely 須改為 truly，且置於動詞 convey 之前；而 public thoughts 須改為 the thoughts of the public。

$$→ \text{Editors'} \begin{cases} \text{opinions} \\ \text{views} \end{cases} \text{can} \begin{cases} \text{truly} \\ \text{accurately} \end{cases} \begin{cases} \text{express} \\ \text{represent} \end{cases}$$

$$\begin{cases} \text{what the public thinks} \\ \text{public opinion} \\ \text{the ideas of the public} \end{cases} \text{in most cases.} 【正】$$

【註釋】 ***of value*** 珍貴的；有價值的（= *valuable*）

proverb〔'prɑvɜb〕*n.* 諺語　　scholar〔'skɑlɚ〕*n.* 學者

not only…but also ~ 不僅…而且~

mouthpiece〔'maʊθ,pis〕*n.* 代言人；發言人

unseen〔ʌn'sin〕*adj.* 看不見的

keep in touch with 和~保持連繫

editor〔'ɛdɪtɚ〕*n.* 編輯　　express〔ɪk'sprɛs〕*v.* 表達

represent〔,rɛprɪ'zɛnt〕*v.* 代表；說明

TEST 4

> 說明：下面一段短文中，有數處係以中文呈現，請利用上下文線索（如單字、片語等）將其譯成正確、通順、達意且前後連貫的英文。

Once upon a time, in a big garden, lived a selfish giant. The garden was beautiful, with green grass, lovely flowers, and singing birds, and children enjoyed playing in it. However, 1. 在巨人決定不讓小孩進入花園，並在花園周圍建造高牆以後， spring never visited the garden. Without the children, it was always winter. The birds would not sing, the flowers felt too sad to bloom, and the trees no longer blossomed. Only the snow, the frost and the wind were happy. It was not until the children crept in through a hole in the wall one day and sang in the trees that the garden came alive again.

2. 巨人終於了解，小孩將春天帶回來了。 His heart melted with joy. And from then on, the giant was always found playing with the children in the most beautiful garden.

1. ....

2. ....

TEST 4 詳解

1. *after the giant decided not let children get into garden, and* *built high walls beside garden,*【誤】（建國中學 陳柏君同學）

   * garden 均須改為 the garden；beside（在~旁邊）須改為 around。

   → after the giant decided $\begin{cases} \text{that he didn't want the} \\ \text{to keep the children} \end{cases}$

   $\left.\begin{array}{l} \text{children in his garden} \\ \text{out of his garden} \end{array}\right\}$ and built a high wall

   around it,【正】

2. *Finally, the giant know that children brought spring back.*【誤】

   （建國中學 陳柏君同學）

   * 依句意為過去式，故動詞 know 須改為 knew。

   → $\left.\begin{array}{l} \text{The giant finally} \\ \text{At last the giant} \end{array}\right\}$ realized that

   $\begin{cases} \text{the children brought back spring.} \\ \text{it was the children that brought spring.} \\ \text{(the) spring would not come back without the children.} \end{cases}$【正】

   【註釋】 ***once upon a time*** 從前（= *long ago*）
   selfish（'sɛlfɪʃ）*adj.* 自私的
   giant（'dʒaɪənt）*n.* 巨人　　bloom（blum）*v.* 開花
   blossom（'blɑsəm）*v.* 開花　　frost（frɔst）*n.* 霜
   creep（krip）*v.* 爬　　***come alive*** 復活
   melt（mɛlt）*v.* 融化　　***from then on*** 從那時起

TEST 5

> 說明：下面一段短文中，有數處係以中文呈現，請利用上下文線索（如單字、片語等）將其譯成正確、通順、達意且前後連貫的英文。

Granny Peach suffered a tragedy, losing family members to suicide. Most of us would have lived in pain and sorrow, but Granny chooses love and courage instead. She does not focus on her worries. Granny says when you can't seem to stop worrying about something, 1. 只要躲在毯子底下，然後所有的煩惱都會消失。 She has seen and accepted the truth that tragedy is a part of life. She says in order for peach trees to produce the best peaches, they need the freezing of the frost, the blasting thunder and the scorching sun. 2. 同樣地，在人生中我們需要辛苦的時刻，才能享受快樂。 The story of Granny Peach and her family is not about tragedy but about love and seeing the beauty of life.

1. ....

2. ....

TEST 5 詳解

1. *as long as you hide under carpet, all the annoyance will disappear.*【誤】(建國中學 許登揚同學)

   * carpet (地毯) 應改成 a blanket (毯子)；annoyance 爲不可數名詞，相當於 worries。

   → just hide under a blanket and then all the worries will
   $$\begin{cases} \text{go away.} \\ \text{disappear.} \end{cases}$$【正】

2. *Similarly, we need hard moment in our life, then we can enjoy happiness.*【誤】(建國中學 許登揚同學)

   * moment 須改爲複數形 moments；then 是副詞，前面須加連接詞 and。

   → $\begin{cases} \text{Likewise,} \\ \text{In the same way,} \\ \text{Similarly,} \end{cases}$ we need $\begin{cases} \text{trying moments} \\ \text{difficult times} \end{cases}$

   in life $\begin{cases} \text{to enjoy happiness.} \\ \text{, and then we can enjoy happiness.} \end{cases}$【正】

【註釋】 suffer (ˈsʌfɚ) v. 遭受　　tragedy (ˈtrædʒədɪ) n. 悲劇
　　　　 suicide (ˈsuəˌsaɪd) n. 自殺　　pain (pen) n. 痛苦
　　　　 sorrow (ˈsɑro) n. 悲傷　　instead (ɪnˈstɛd) adv. 作爲代替
　　　　 in order for ~ to V. 爲了讓~…　　peach (pitʃ) n. 桃子
　　　　 freezing (ˈfrizɪŋ) n. 冷凍；結冰　　frost (frɔst) n. 霜
　　　　 blasting (ˈblæstɪŋ) adj. 發出巨響的
　　　　 thunder (ˈθʌndɚ) n. 雷　　scorching (ˈskɔrtʃɪŋ) adj. 酷熱的
　　　　 blanket (ˈblæŋkɪt) n. 毯子　　likewise (ˈlaɪkˌwaɪz) adv. 同樣地
　　　　 trying (ˈtraɪɪŋ) adj. 辛苦的；難熬的

TEST 6

Mark, a twenty-two-year-old boy, graduates from university. He thinks he has grown up and that he is old enough to decide everything by himself. However, in his parents' eyes, he is still a kid, 1. 而且他們習慣於為他安排一切。 All that they want him to do is follow their advice. That's how the conflict begins. Mark, who has lots of pressure and complaints, cannot endure it anymore. Therefore, he writes to an advice columnist, asking for help, because he really does not know what to do. Finally, 2. 專欄作家建議他和父母溝通 and let them know his life goal. Maybe they will find Mark is an adult and that they should allow him to plan for his future on his own.

1. ....

2. ....

TEST 6 詳解

1. *and they are used to arrange everything for him.* 【誤】

（北一女中　王瑜蕙同學）

* be used to + V-ing「習慣於…」，故 arrange 須改爲 arranging。

$$\rightarrow \text{and they are} \left\{ \begin{array}{l} \text{used to} \\ \text{accustomed to} \\ \text{in the habit of} \end{array} \right\} \left\{ \begin{array}{l} \text{arranging} \\ \text{organizing} \end{array} \right\}$$

everything for him. 【正】

2. *…suggests him to communicate with his parents* 【誤】

（北一女中　王瑜蕙同學）

* 句首應寫出 the columnist（專欄作家）；suggests him to communicate 須改爲 suggests that he communicate。

$$\rightarrow \text{the columnist} \left\{ \begin{array}{l} \text{suggests} \\ \text{recommends} \end{array} \right\} \text{that he communicate}$$

with his parents 【正】

【註釋】 graduate〔'grædʒʊ,et〕v. 畢業　　**grow up** 長大
by oneself 靠自己　　follow〔'falo〕v. 聽從
advice〔əd'vaɪs〕n. 忠告；建議
conflict〔'kɑnflɪkt〕n. 衝突
pressure〔'prɛʃɚ〕n. 壓力
complaint〔kəm'plent〕n. 抱怨
endure〔ɪn'djʊr〕v. 忍受　　**not…anymore** 不再…
columnist〔'kɑləmnɪst〕n. 專欄作家
goal〔gol〕n. 目標　　**on one's own** 靠自己；獨自

TEST 7

I am a senior high student. I am fifteen, and have to share a room with my nine-year-old brother. He is very naughty and untidy. He always makes our room messy, and never leaves my stuff alone. 1.他一直開我的櫃子，看裡面的所有東西。 Nothing I have is private. Also, I am not allowed to do what I like to do. For example, 2.我晚上必須把我的收音機關掉，因為噪音會使他睡不著。 Mom always says that I must love and take care of my younger brother because he is the only brother I have.

1. ⋯⋯⋯⋯⋯⋯⋯⋯⋯⋯⋯⋯⋯⋯⋯⋯⋯⋯⋯⋯⋯⋯⋯⋯

2. ⋯⋯⋯⋯⋯⋯⋯⋯⋯⋯⋯⋯⋯⋯⋯⋯⋯⋯⋯⋯⋯⋯⋯⋯

TEST 7 詳解

1. *He keep on opening my closet, see all the things inside.* 【誤】

（中正高中 呂政哲同學）

* keep 須改爲 keeps；see 須改爲 and looking at。

→ He keeps opening my closet and looking at

$$\begin{cases} \text{everything inside.} \\ \text{the things inside it.} \end{cases} 【正】$$

2. *I need to turn off my radio at night, because the noise will make him awake.* 【誤】 （中正高中 呂政哲同學）

* make him awake 應改爲 keep him awake。

$$→ I \begin{cases} \text{have to} \\ \text{must} \end{cases} \begin{cases} \text{turn my radio off} \\ \text{turn off my radio} \end{cases} \text{at night because}$$

$$\text{the noise} \begin{cases} \text{keeps him awake.} \\ \text{prevents him} \\ \text{stops him} \end{cases} \text{from sleeping.} 【正】$$

【註釋】 share〔ʃɛr〕*v.* 分享；共有

naughty〔'nɔtɪ〕*adj.* 頑皮的

untidy〔ʌn'taɪdɪ〕*adj.* 不整潔的

messy〔'mɛsɪ〕*adj.* 雜亂的

leave~alone 不打擾~　　stuff〔stʌf〕*n.* 東西

private〔'praɪvɪt〕*adj.* 私人的　　*take care of* 照顧

closet〔'klɑzɪt〕*n.* 衣櫥；衣櫃

turn off 關掉（電源）　　awake〔ə'wek〕*adj.* 醒著的

TEST 8

說明：下面一段短文中，有數處係以中文呈現，請利用上下文線索（如單字、片語等）將其譯成正確、通順、達意且前後連貫的英文。

A boy threw a stone onto the roof of a lady's house by accident. 1. 他怕被抓到，所以他立刻離開。 For the next few days, he felt sorry for what he had done and decided to save the money he made from delivering newspapers to pay the cost of repairing her window. In three weeks, 2. 他把錢準備好，並且和一張紙條一起放入一個信封裡， which said that he was sorry for breaking the window and that he hoped that the money would cover the cost.

1. ....

2. ....

TEST 8 詳解

1. *He was afraid of being catch, so he ran away immediately.*【誤】

（中山女中 楊佳穎同學）

* catch 須改為過去分詞 caught。

→ He was afraid of being caught, so he $\begin{cases} \text{took off} \\ \text{left} \\ \text{ran away} \end{cases}$

$\begin{cases} \text{without delay.} \\ \text{immediately.} \\ \text{right away.} \\ \text{at once.} \end{cases}$ 【正】

2. *he had prepared money already, and put into an envolope with a piece of paper,*【誤】（中山女中 楊佳穎同學）

* put into 須加受詞，寫成 put it into；envolope 拼錯，須改為 envelope（信封）。

→ he had the money ready and $\begin{cases} \text{put} \\ \text{placed} \end{cases}$ it in an

envelope $\begin{cases} \text{with} \\ \text{along with} \\ \text{together with} \end{cases}$ a note, 【正】

【註釋】 onto（'ɑntə）*prep.* 到…上面　　roof（ruf）*n.* 屋頂
by accident 意外地；偶然地　　save（sev）*v.* 存（錢）
deliver（dɪ'lɪvɚ）*v.* 遞送　　cost（kɔst）*n.* 費用
repair（rɪ'pɛr）*v.* 修理　　cover（'kʌvɚ）*v.* 足夠支付
take off 離開　　*without delay* 立刻
envelope（'ɛnvə,lop）*n.* 信封　　note（not）*n.* 紙條

TEST 9

說明：下面一段短文中，有數處係以中文呈現，請利用上下文線索（如單字、片語等）將其譯成正確、通順、達意且前後連貫的英文。

The statue of the Happy Prince stood in the middle of the city. His body was covered in gold, and he had two jewels for eyes. Another jewel was in the handle of his sword. One night, a little bird flew into the city. 1. 他正在往南的途中，因為冬天就要來了。 The bird decided to rest between the feet of the Happy Prince. Just as he was settling in, something strange happened. A drop of water landed on his head, and then another. He looked up and saw that the Happy Prince was crying. The bird asked why he was crying and 2. 王子說，他一直過著快樂的生活，但他現在所看到的，都是痛苦和醜陋的東西。

1. ....

2. ....

TEST 9 詳解

1. *He was on the way to South because the winter was coming.* 【誤】

（景美女中 殷偉珊同學）

* to South 須改成 south 或 to the south。

→ He was $\begin{cases} \text{on his way south} \\ \text{going south} \\ \text{flying south} \end{cases}$ because $\begin{cases} \text{the winter} \\ \text{winter} \end{cases}$

was $\begin{cases} \text{approaching.} \\ \text{coming.} \end{cases}$ 【正】

2. *the prince said he led a happy life but what he saw was painful and ugly things.* 【誤】（景美女中 殷偉珊同學）

* 須將 led 改為 had led，因為比過去的動作早發生，須用「過去完成式」。

→ the prince said that he had $\begin{cases} \text{lived} \\ \text{had} \end{cases}$ a happy life,

but $\begin{cases} \text{all he saw now was} \\ \text{now he only saw} \end{cases}$ pain and ugly things. 【正】

【註釋】　statue (ˈstætʃʊ) *n.* 雕像　　prince (prɪns) *n.* 王子

cover (ˈkʌvɚ) *v.* 覆蓋　　jewel (ˈdʒuəl) *n.* 珠寶

sword (sord) *n.* 劍　　rest (rɛst) *v.* 休息

settle in 安居；安頓下來　　***land on*** 落在

on *one's* ***way*** 在去～的途中

south (sauθ) *adv.* 往南　*n.* 南方

approach (əˈprotʃ) *v.* 接近

pain (pen) *n.* 痛苦　　ugly (ˈʌglɪ) *adj.* 醜陋的

TEST 10

> 說明：下面一段短文中，有數處係以中文呈現，請利用上下文線索（如單字、片語等）將其譯成正確、通順、達意且前後連貫的英文。

Have you ever been sick with a cold? If so, you probably noticed your body getting really hot. 1.當我們生病時，身體產生的這種熱，就叫作發燒。 Fevers may make us feel uncomfortable but, in fact, they are good for us. They fight the tiny things that have entered our bodies and made us sick.

As soon as we get sick, the brain raises the body's temperature to kill the sickness. This makes our bodies ache and makes us feel hot. 2.吃藥來退燒就意味著，我們的身體必須更努力才能康復。 So, the next time you have a low fever, don't worry. Drink lots of water and go lie down. Your fever is a sign that your body is working hard to keep you healthy.

1. ....

2. ....

TEST 10　詳解

1. <u>*When we are sick, the heat our bodies produce is so called*</u>
   <u>*fever.*</u>【誤】（建國中學　許登揚同學）

   * is so called fever 須改爲 is called a fever，因爲 fever 是可數名詞，
   又 so-called 是指「所謂的」。

   → This heat $\begin{cases} \text{that the body produces} \\ \text{produced} \\ \text{made} \end{cases}$ by the body

   when we are $\begin{cases} \text{sick} \\ \text{ill} \end{cases}$ is called a fever.　【正】

2. <u>*Having medicine…means that our bodies have to make more*</u>
   <u>*effort to recover.*</u>【誤】（建國中學　許登揚同學）

   *「吃藥」動詞須用 take，故須將 Having 改成 Taking；「退燒」是
   lower the fever。

   → Taking medicine to $\begin{cases} \text{lower} \\ \text{reduce} \end{cases}$ the fever means our

   bodies $\begin{cases} \text{have to} \\ \text{must} \end{cases}$ work harder to $\begin{cases} \text{get well.} \\ \text{recover.} \end{cases}$　【正】

   【註釋】 ***be sick with*** 罹患　　cold〔kold〕*n.* 感冒
   　　　　notice〔'notɪs〕*v.* 注意到　　fever〔'fivɚ〕*n.* 發燒
   　　　　fight〔faɪt〕*v.* 與…作戰　　tiny〔'taɪnɪ〕*adj.* 微小的
   　　　　raise〔rez〕*v.* 提高　　ache〔ek〕*v.* 疼痛
   　　　　sign〔saɪn〕*n.* 徵兆；跡象
   　　　　healthy〔'hɛlθɪ〕*adj.* 健康的　　lower〔'loɚ〕*v.* 降低
   　　　　get well 康復　　recover〔rɪ'kʌvɚ〕*v.* 康復

TEST 11

　　1.保護我們的環境是很重要的，而最好的方法之一，就是節約用水。 Water is one of the most valuable resources on our planet. Sadly, the world's supply of water is under threat. People have grown used to wasting water, and changes in the global climate mean that droughts and water rationing are becoming increasingly common. However, we can make a difference. 2.我們應該盡力節約用水、節約能源，以及拯救我們的地球。

1. ....

2. ....

TEST 11 詳解

1. <u>*Protecting our environment is very important, and one of the*</u> <u>*best ways is preserving water.*</u>【誤】（建國中學 林浩存同學）

* preserving（保存）須改爲 conserving（節省）。

$$\rightarrow \left\{ \begin{array}{l} \text{It is important to protect our environment} \\ \text{Protecting our environment is important} \end{array} \right\}$$

and $\left\{ \begin{array}{l} \text{one of the best ways is to conserve water.} \\ \text{saving water is one of the best ways.} \end{array} \right.$ 【正】

2. <u>*We should make efforts to save water and energy to save the*</u> <u>*earth.*</u>【誤】（建國中學 林浩存同學）

* 須將 make efforts（努力）改成 do our best（盡力）；save water and energy to save the earth 應改成 save water, energy, and the earth。

$$\rightarrow \text{We} \left\{ \begin{array}{l} \text{should} \\ \text{ought to} \end{array} \right\} \left\{ \begin{array}{l} \text{try our best} \\ \text{do all we can} \end{array} \right\} \text{to save water,}$$

energy, and $\left\{ \begin{array}{l} \text{our planet.} \\ \text{the planet.} \quad\text{【正】} \\ \text{the earth.} \end{array} \right.$

【註釋】　valuable〔'væljυəbl̞〕*adj.* 珍貴的　　resource〔rɪ'sors〕*n.* 資源
　　　　　planet〔'plænɪt〕*n.* 行星（在此指「地球」）
　　　　　sadly〔'sædlɪ〕*adv.* 可悲的是　　supply〔sə'plaɪ〕*n.* 供給
　　　　　threat〔θrɛt〕*n.* 威脅　　***be under threat*** 受到威脅
　　　　　grow used to V-ing 變得習慣於～
　　　　　global〔'globl̞〕*adj.* 全球的　　drought〔draυt〕*n.* 乾旱
　　　　　water rationing 限水　　increasingly〔ɪn'krisɪŋlɪ〕*adv.* 越來越
　　　　　make a difference 有影響　　conserve〔kən'sɜv〕*v.* 節省

TEST 12

說明：下面一段短文中，有數處係以中文呈現，請利用上下
　　　文線索（如單字、片語等）將其譯成正確、通順、達
　　　意且前後連貫的英文。

Those who are lazy may be reluctant to admit it, but the human brain is like a machine in many ways. That is to say, the more you use it, the more it works. 1.如果你儘可能經常使用它，你就會有良好的記憶力。 Doctor says that you must exercise your brain with new activities from time to time; otherwise, it will easily grow lazy. One way to stimulate your brain is to learn new skills, such as tennis, knitting, and driving. Another way is to build up your vocabulary by reading extensively. If you familiarize yourself with more words, 2.當你需要它們時，你會比較容易想起它們。

1. ......

2. ......

TEST 12 詳解

1. <u>*If you use it as much as you can, you will have good*</u>
   <u>*memory.*</u>【誤】（中山女中 董怡萱同學）

   * memory（記憶力）為可數名詞，故前面須加 a。

   → Use it as often as possible, and you will have a good
      memory.【正】

   或 If you use it as much as you can, you will have a
      good memory.【正】

2. <u>*when you need them, you will think up with them more easily.*</u>【誤】

   （中山女中 董怡萱同學）

   * think up with them 須改為 think them up（想起它們）。

   → it will be easier for you to
   $\left\{ \begin{array}{l} \text{recall} \\ \text{remember} \end{array} \right\}$ them when

   $\left\{ \begin{array}{l} \text{you need them.} \\ \text{necessary.} \end{array} \right.$ 【正】

   【註釋】 lazy（'lezɪ）*adj.* 懶惰的
   　　　　reluctant（rɪ'lʌktənt）*adj.* 不情願的
   　　　　admit（əd'mɪt）*v.* 承認　　way（we）*n.* 方面
   　　　　that is to say 也就是說　　***from time to time*** 時常
   　　　　grow（gro）*v.* 變得　　stimulate（'stɪmjə,let）*v.* 刺激
   　　　　skill（skɪl）*n.* 技能　　knitting（'nɪtɪŋ）*n.* 編織
   　　　　build up 增加；累積　　vocabulary（və'kæbjə,lɛrɪ）*n.* 字彙
   　　　　extensively（ɪk'stɛnsɪvlɪ）*adv.* 廣泛地
   　　　　familiarize（fə'mɪljə,raɪz）*v.* 使熟悉
   　　　　memory（'mɛmərɪ）*n.* 記憶力
   　　　　recall（rɪ'kɔl）*v.* 記得；想起

TEST 13

Advertising has gradually taught most of us to have a questioning attitude about what we see in television commercials. 1. 我們理所當然會認為，產品可能不像廠商聲稱的那麼好， and that the detergent does not take out every dirty spot immediately without a lot of hard work. And you know you will never become a star tennis player just by wearing a certain kind of tennis shoe. The shoes may, though, turn out to be a well-made brand that will improve the quality of your tennis game. In any case, 2. 明智的人會質疑他們從廣告商那裡獲得的資訊 and do not assume it is accurate.

1. ....

2. ....

TEST 13 詳解

1. <u>*We take it for granted that the product may not be as good as the manufactory has claimed,*</u> 【误】（中山女中 盧胤諮同學）

* manufactory 須改爲 manufacturer（廠商）。

→ We take it for granted that a product may not be as good as the manufacturer $\begin{cases} \text{claims,} \\ \text{says it is,} \end{cases}$ 【正】

2. <u>*wise people will suspect the information that they get from the advertisement*</u> 【误】（中山女中 盧胤諮同學）

* 須將 advertisement（廣告）改爲 advertisers（廣告商）。

→ $\begin{cases} \text{sensible} \\ \text{rational} \\ \text{smart} \end{cases}$ people $\begin{cases} \text{question} \\ \text{are suspicious of} \end{cases}$ the information they receive from advertisers 【正】

【註釋】 advertising（ˈædvɚˌtaɪzɪŋ）n. 廣告
gradually（ˈgrædʒʊəlɪ）adv. 逐漸地
questioning（ˈkwɛstʃənɪŋ）adj. 質疑的
commercial（kəˈmɝʃəl）n. 商業廣告
detergent（dɪˈtɝdʒənt）n. 清潔劑；洗衣粉   spot（spɑt）n. 點
certain（ˈsɝtn̩）adj. 某個   *turn out to be* 結果是
brand（brænd）n. 品牌   *in any case* 無論如何
assume（əˈsjum）v. 認定   accurate（ˈækjərɪt）adj. 準確的
take it for granted that~ 視~爲理所當然
manufacturer（ˌmænjəˈfæktʃərɚ）n. 廠商   claim（klem）v. 宣稱
sensible（ˈsɛnsəbl̩）adj. 明智的   question（ˈkwɛstʃən）v. 質疑
advertiser（ˈædvɚˌtaɪzɚ）n. 刊登廣告者

TEST 14

説明：下面一段短文中，有數處係以中文呈現，請利用上下文線索（如單字、片語等）將其譯成正確、通順、達意且前後連貫的英文。

When people are under stress they react in different ways. 1. <u>有些人覺得很難保持冷靜，而且常會變得很緊張。</u> Little things, like a baby crying, can make them irritated. They get very annoyed if they have to wait just a few minutes too long in a shop or a restaurant. These people are usually very moody. One minute they are fine and the next they can be absolutely furious. Other people seem to stay calm almost all the time, and rarely get angry. For example, 2. <u>如果他們遇到塞車，他們不會生氣。</u> They sit calmly in their cars, telling themselves that there is nothing they can do about the situation.

1. ....

2. ....

TEST 14 詳解

1. *Some people think it's hard to calm down, and often become neverous.* 【誤】（萬芳高中 黃致文同學）

   * 「保持冷靜」須寫成 stay calm；而 neverous 拼錯，須改為 nervous（緊張的）。

   → Some people find it $\left\{ \begin{array}{l} \text{difficult} \\ \text{hard} \end{array} \right\}$ to stay calm

   and $\left\{ \begin{array}{l} \text{often} \\ \text{they often} \end{array} \right\}$ become $\left\{ \begin{array}{l} \text{nervous.} \\ \text{tense.} \end{array} \right\}$ 【正】

2. *if they encounter car jam, they won't get angry.* 【誤】

   （萬芳高中 黃致文同學）

   * 「塞車」是 a traffic jam。

   → if they $\left\{ \begin{array}{l} \text{are} \\ \text{get} \end{array} \right\}$ caught in $\left\{ \begin{array}{l} \text{bad traffic} \\ \text{a traffic jam} \\ \text{traffic congestion} \end{array} \right\}$,

   they don't get $\left\{ \begin{array}{l} \text{angry.} \\ \text{upset.} \end{array} \right\}$ 【正】

【註釋】 stress〔strɛs〕*n.* 壓力　　react〔rɪˋækt〕*v.* 反應
irritated〔ˋɪrəˌtetɪd〕*adj.* 被激怒的；生氣的
get〔gɛt〕*v.* 變得　　annoyed〔əˋnɔɪd〕*adj.* 惱怒的
moody〔ˋmudɪ〕*adj.* 情緒化的
absolutely〔ˋæbsəˌlutlɪ〕*adv.* 完全地
furious〔ˋfjʊrɪəs〕*adj.* 狂怒的　　rarely〔ˋrɛrlɪ〕*adv.* 很少
nervous〔ˋnɝvəs〕*adj.* 緊張的　　tense〔tɛns〕*adj.* 緊張的
be caught in 遇到（= *get caught in*）
upset〔ʌpˋsɛt〕*adj.* 不高興的

TEST 15

Tornadoes are funnels of air rotating as fast as 300 miles per hour. <u>1. 它們是具有破壞性以及無法預測的風暴。</u> Spring and summer are the time when tornadoes occur most often. Although scientists know a great deal about tornadoes, <u>2. 他們仍然無法斷定它們會在何時及何地形成。</u> The path of a tornado is hard to predict. It can turn quickly as well as move in a straight line. Fortunately, not all tornadoes are so dangerous. Many are small storms that form quickly and disappear, causing little or no damage.

1. ....

2. ....

TEST 15 詳解

1. _They are destroytive and unpredictable…_【誤】（永春高中 董巧儀同學）

* destroytive 須改成 destructive（破壞性的），句尾應寫出 windstorms（風暴）。

→ They are $\left\{\begin{array}{l}\text{destructive}\\\text{devastating}\end{array}\right\}$ and unpredictable

   windstorms.【正】

2. _they still couldn't decide when or where they will form._【誤】

（永春高中 董巧儀同學）

* 依句意為現在式，須將 couldn't 改成 can't。

→ they still can't determine when and where they

   will form.【正】

【註釋】 tornado〔tɔr'nedo〕n. 龍捲風

funnel〔'fʌnḷ〕n. 漏斗

rotate〔'rotet〕v. 旋轉　　per〔pɚ〕prep. 每

a great deal 很多　　path〔pæθ〕n. 路徑

predict〔prɪ'dɪkt〕v. 預測

as well as 以及　　straight〔stret〕adj. 直的

cause〔kɔz〕v. 造成

destructive〔dɪ'strʌktɪv〕adj. 破壞性的

devastating〔'dɛvəs,tetɪŋ〕adj. 破壞性的

unpredictable〔,ʌnprɪ'dɪktəbḷ〕adj. 無法預測的

windstorm〔'wɪnd,stɔrm〕n. 風暴

determine〔dɪ'tɝmɪn〕v. 斷定

TEST 16

> 說明：下面一段短文中，有數處係以中文呈現，請利用上下
> 文線索（如單字、片語等）將其譯成正確、通順、達
> 意且前後連貫的英文。

The Grand Hotel looks like a Chinese palace. It's a 5-star hotel that provides its guests with great service. The hotel is a grand building with 12 floors. Each floor shows different parts of Chinese history and art. Each room is different. 1. 你越往上，房間就越舒適。 Many rooms have a balcony. Guests can enjoy a magnificent view of Taipei city from the balcony. The hotel also has six restaurants. Visitors can have celebrations at the hotel, too. 2. 它有特殊的房間，供派對與宴會使用。 No wonder so many guests enjoy their stay in the Grand Hotel.

1. ....

2. ....

TEST 16 詳解

1. *The higher you go, the comfortabler the room will be.*【誤】

   * comfortable 的比較級是 more comfortable。

   → The higher up you go, the more comfortable the
   rooms are. 【正】

2. *It has special room for party and banquet.*【誤】

   * room、party 和 banquet 都是可數名詞，故都必須在字尾加 s。

   → $\left\{ \begin{array}{l} \text{It has} \\ \text{There are} \end{array} \right\}$ special rooms for parties

   and banquets. 【正】

   【註釋】 grand〔grænd〕*adj.* 宏偉的
   　　　　Grand Hotel 圓山飯店　　palace〔'pælɪs〕*n.* 宮殿
   　　　　floor〔flor〕*n.* 樓層
   　　　　balcony〔'bælkənɪ〕*n.* 陽台
   　　　　magnificent〔mæg'nɪfəsṇt〕*adj.* 壯麗的
   　　　　view〔vju〕*n.* 景色
   　　　　celebration〔‚sɛlə'breʃən〕*n.* 慶祝活動
   　　　　no wonder 難怪　　stay〔ste〕*n.* 暫住
   　　　　banquet〔'bæŋkwɪt〕*n.* 宴會；盛宴

TEST 17

說明：下面一段短文中，有數處係以中文呈現，請利用上下文線索（如單字、片語等）將其譯成正確、通順、達意且前後連貫的英文。

Taiwan was once called "Formosa," the beautiful island. Taiwan offers a lot of wonderful tourist attractions. The more places you visit in Taiwan, the more opportunities you will have to realize how beautiful it is. Instead of traveling abroad, 1.有越來越多的台灣人，去台灣值得一遊的地方。

In addition, our beautiful scenery also attracts more than 1.5 million tourists from around the world. There are two main reasons. One is that Taiwan has a variety of sights to explore, ranging from towering mountains to excellent coastal spots. 2.另一個理由是，台灣人很好客。 As tourists experience the beauty of Taiwan, they will receive a warm welcome from friendly people wherever they go.

1. ....

2. ....

TEST 17 詳解

1. <u>*more and more Taiwanese are going to the place which is*</u>
   <u>*worthy to visit in Taiwan.*</u>【誤】（北一女中 林貝瑄同學）

   * in Taiwan 須移至 place 之後；is worthy to visit 須改爲 is worth
   visiting 或 is worth a visit (值得一遊)。

   $$\rightarrow \left.\begin{array}{l}\text{more and more} \\ \text{an increasing number of}\end{array}\right\} \text{Taiwanese go to places}$$

   $$\text{in Taiwan that} \left\{\begin{array}{l}\text{deserve a visit.} \\ \text{are worth visiting.}\end{array}\right. 【正】$$

2. <u>*The other reason is Taiwanese are passionate.*</u>【誤】（北一女中 林貝瑄同學）

   * 須將 passionate (熱情的) 改爲 hospitable (好客的)。

   → Another reason is the hospitality of (the) Taiwanese
   people. 【正】

   或 The hospitality of (the) Taiwanese people is another
   reason. 【正】

   【註釋】 ***tourist attraction*** 觀光景點 ***instead of*** 不…而~
   abroad〔ə'brɔd〕*adv.* 到國外
   in addition 此外 scenery〔'sinərɪ〕*n.* 風景
   a variety of 各種的；各式各樣的
   explore〔ɪk'splor〕*v.* 探索
   range from A ***to*** B (範圍) 從 A 到 B 都有
   coastal〔'kostḷ〕*adj.* 海岸的 spot〔spat〕*n.* 景點
   experience〔ɪk'spɪrɪəns〕*v.* 體驗 deserve〔dɪ'zɝv〕*v.* 值得
   hospitality〔ˌhaspɪ'tælətɪ〕*n.* 好客

TEST 18

That night, I found myself lying awake long after she left. I regretted that I hadn't told her how sorry I was. I still haven't forgotten what happened. Now my own children are all grown-up and gone and I often go next door to spend the night with her. <u>1. 在某個感恩節前夕，當時我幾乎快睡著了，</u> my mom came to brush the hair from my forehead and kissed me just like before. Catching her hand in mine, I finally told her I was sorry. To my surprise, my mom didn't know what I was talking about — <u>2. 她早就已經既往不咎了。</u>

1. ....

2. ....

TEST 18 詳解

1. *One Thanksgiving eve, when I almost fallen asleep,*【誤】

（延平高中 葉家亨同學）

* 須將 I almost fallen 改成過去完成式 I had almost fallen。

$$\rightarrow \begin{cases} \text{On one Thanksgiving Eve,} \\ \text{One night, the night before Thanksgiving,} \end{cases}$$

$$\begin{cases} \text{when I had almost fallen asleep,} \\ \text{just as I was falling asleep,} \end{cases} \text{【正】}$$

2. *she has already didn't mind anyway.*【誤】（延平高中 葉家亨同學）

* 「既往不咎」是 forgive and forget，在此為過去完成式，故須改成 had forgiven and forgotten。

$$\rightarrow \text{she had} \begin{cases} \text{already forgiven and} \\ \text{forgiven me long ago and} \end{cases}$$

$$\begin{cases} \text{forgotten.} \\ \text{did not even remember it.} \end{cases} \text{【正】}$$

【註釋】 lie〔laɪ〕v. 躺著　　awake〔əˈwek〕adj. 醒著的
regret〔rɪˈgrɛt〕v. 後悔
grown-up〔ˈgronˌʌp〕adj. 長大的　　brush〔brʌʃ〕v. 梳
forehead〔ˈforˌhɛd〕n. 前額
to one's surprise 令某人驚訝的是
Thanksgiving〔ˌθæŋksˈgɪvɪŋ〕n. 感恩節（11 月的第四個禮拜四）
eve〔iv〕n. 前夕　　*fall asleep* 睡著
forgive and forget 既往不咎

TEST 19

說明：下面一段短文中，有數處係以中文呈現，請利用上下
文線索（如單字、片語等）將其譯成正確、通順、達
意且前後連貫的英文。

In ancient times, salt was such an important item on
the dining table that it had to be placed in front of the
king when he sat to eat. Important guests at the king's
table were seated near the salt. <u>1. 較不重要的客人，會坐在
離它較遠的位子。</u>

In the early days in the United States, salt was very
hard to get. Little did people know that there was enough
salt under the ground. <u>2. 當時賣鹽的商店老闆會非常小心處
理他的鹽。</u> As he poured out salt for a customer, he
would stop anyone from walking across the floor of the
store. If there was any shaking of the floor, it could
cause the salt to "settle". As a result, the storekeeper
would have to add a little more salt to the amount he
had already poured out.

1. ....

2. ....

TEST 19 詳解

1. _Less important guests were seated far from it._【誤】

（北一女中 龔哲儀同學）

* 「離～較遠」須用比較級，故 far from 須改為 farther away from。

→ {
Less important guests
Guests that were not so important
} were

{
given seats
seated
} farther away from it.【正】

2. _The storekeeper sold salt at that time deal with his salt carefully._【誤】（師大附中 邱懷瑩同學）

* The storekeeper 須改為 A storekeeper who；依句意為過去式，故 deal 須改為 dealt。

→ A storekeeper who sold salt {
at that time
then
}

was very careful with it.【正】

【註釋】 _in ancient times_ 在古代　　salt〔sɔlt〕_n._ 鹽

item〔'aɪtəm〕_n._ 物品　　_dining table_ 餐桌

place〔ples〕_v._ 放　　_be seated_ 就座；入座

pour〔por〕_v._ 傾倒

stop sb. from V-ing 使某人不要～

cause〔kɔz〕_v._ 使　　settle〔'sɛtl̩〕_v._ 下沈；沈澱

as a result 因此　　_add A to B_ 把 A 加到 B

TEST 20

說明：下面一段短文中，有數處係以中文呈現，請利用上下
　　　文線索（如單字、片語等）將其譯成正確、通順、達
　　　意且前後連貫的英文。

Curtis was not feeling well. He had a headache and a stomachache, and was feeling tired. He was a bit worried when he looked in the mirror and saw his appearance. He looked old and sick, 1. 就好像他罹患了某種慢性病。 He thought he had better see a doctor.

The doctor asked Curtis about his eating and sleeping habits, and then told him he was getting too little sleep. The doctor also said Curtis had a slight infection. It was very common, and the treatment was a simple injection. Curtis was nervous about having a needle stuck into his arm, 2. 但是當他發現一點也不痛時，他鬆了一口氣。 The doctor said he would soon get better and told him to go home.

1. ....

2. ....

TEST 20　詳解

1. *as if he was suffer from a chronic disease.* 【誤】（大同高中　謝家惠同學）

　　* suffer 須改為 suffering。

$$\rightarrow \left.\begin{array}{l} \text{as if} \\ \text{as though} \end{array}\right\} \text{he} \left\{\begin{array}{l} \text{was suffering from} \\ \text{had} \end{array}\right\} \text{a}$$

$$\text{chronic} \left\{\begin{array}{l} \text{disease.} \\ \text{illness.} \end{array}\right. \text{【正】}$$

2. *but when he found out that it was not hurt at all, he relieved.* 【誤】

（大同高中　謝家惠同學）

　　*「會痛」是 hurt 而不是 be hurt（受傷）;「鬆了一口氣」須將 relieved
　　改成 was relieved。

　　→ but was relieved when he found it didn't

$$\left\{\begin{array}{l} \text{hurt at all.} \\ \text{cause him any pain.} \end{array}\right. \text{【正】}$$

【註釋】　stomachache (ˈstʌmək͵ek) n. 胃痛
　　　　　mirror (ˈmɪrɚ) n. 鏡子
　　　　　appearance (əˈpɪrəns) n. 外表；樣子
　　　　　slight (slaɪt) adj. 輕微的　　infection (ɪnˈfɛkʃən) n. 感染
　　　　　treatment (ˈtritmənt) n. 治療方式
　　　　　injection (ɪnˈdʒɛkʃən) n. 注射
　　　　　nervous (ˈnɝvəs) adj. 緊張的　　needle (ˈnidḷ) n. 針
　　　　　stick (stɪk) v. 刺　　*suffer from* 罹患
　　　　　chronic (ˈkrɑnɪk) adj. 慢性的
　　　　　relieved (rɪˈlivd) adj. 鬆了一口氣的　　hurt (hɝt) v. 痛

TEST 21

Just remember that foreigners are not that much different from Chinese people.　What we can talk about depends on how well we know a person.　When we first meet, 1. 最好談論一些我們很確定我們擁有的共同話題。　That's why so many people talk about the weather when they want to start a conversation. Other "safe" topics might include 2. 時事、運動、我們看過的電影以及我們喜歡的音樂。　As we get to know a person better, we can begin to talk about more personal topics.

1. ....

2. ....

TEST 21 詳解

1. *we had better talk about some conversations that we're sure that we both have.* 【誤】

   * 須將 conversations (對話) 改為 topics (話題)，we both have 須改為 we have in common (我們共同擁有的)。

   → it's better to talk about topics we're sure that we have in common. 【正】

2. *latest news, sports, the movies we've seen and our favorite musics.* 【誤】

   * latest news 前須加 the，且 musics 須改為 music。

   → current $\begin{cases} \text{events} \\ \text{affairs} \end{cases}$, sports, movies we've seen, and music we like. 【正】

   【註釋】 foreigner (ˈfɔrɪnɚ) *n.* 外國人
   　　　　 depend on 視~而定
   　　　　 include (ɪnˈklud) *v.* 包括　　***get to*** 得以
   　　　　 personal (ˈpɝsn̩l) *adj.* 個人的；私人的
   　　　　 in common 共同的
   　　　　 current (ˈkɝənt) *adj.* 目前的
   　　　　 current events 時事 (= *current affairs*)

TEST 22

> 說明：下面一段短文中，有數處係以中文呈現，請利用上下
> 文線索（如單字、片語等）將其譯成正確、通順、達
> 意且前後連貫的英文。

As the population of the world gets larger and larger, people wonder whether farmers can provide everyone with enough food. Since the first biopesticide was developed in 1961, farmers in the west have produced nearly a quarter more food per person at a cost 40 percent lower than before. To supplement the traditional ways of producing more food, 1.科學家藉由改變它們的基因物質，而研發出較強韌的植物。 Foods from such plants are called GM foods, and they are believed to be the best answer to the problem of feeding the world's growing population. However, GM plants are not absolutely perfect. Since they are unnatural, some even think they might do us harm. Actually, no one knows how good or bad these foods may be for human beings. In a word, 2.基因改造食物開始扮演一個重要但有爭議的角色 in feeding the world's growing population.

1. ....

2. ....

TEST 22 詳解

1. *by changing their genetic substances, scientists have created tougher plants.*【誤】（師大附中 游智勝同學）

   * genetic material（基因物質）是固定説法，不可寫成 *genetic substances*（誤）。

   → scientists have $\left\{ \begin{array}{l} \text{developed} \\ \text{created} \end{array} \right\}$ $\left\{ \begin{array}{l} \text{stronger} \\ \text{hardier} \end{array} \right\}$ plants

   by $\left\{ \begin{array}{l} \text{changing} \\ \text{altering} \end{array} \right\}$ their genetic material.【正】

2. *GM food has begun to play an important but conventional role*【誤】（師大附中 游智勝同學）

   * 應將 conventional（傳統的）改成 controversial（有爭議的）。

   → GM foods are starting to play an important but

   controversial $\left\{ \begin{array}{l} \text{role} \\ \text{part} \end{array} \right\}$【正】

【註釋】 population (ˌpɑpjəˈleʃən) *n.* 人口
wonder (ˈwʌndə) *v.* 想知道
biopesticide (ˌbaɪəˈpɛstəˌsaɪd) *n.* 生物殺蟲劑
develop (dɪˈvɛləp) *v.* 研發　***a quarter*** 四分之一
traditional (trəˈdɪʃənḷ) *adj.* 傳統的
GM *adj.* 基因改造的（ = *genetically modified* ）
answer (ˈænsə) *n.* 對策　　feed (fid) *v.* 給（人）食物
absolutely (ˈæbsəˌlutlɪ) *adv.* 完全地
actually (ˈæktʃʊəlɪ) *adv.* 事實上　***human beings*** 人類
hardy (ˈhɑrdɪ) *adj.* 耐寒的　　genetic (dʒəˈnɛtɪk) *adj.* 基因的
controversial (ˌkɑntrəˈvɜʃəl) *adj.* 有爭議的

TEST 23

說明：下面一段短文中，有數處係以中文呈現，請利用上下文線索（如單字、片語等）將其譯成正確、通順、達意且前後連貫的英文。

   Everyone knows that a mother's love is unconditional and it is totally selfless. <u>1.母親只是不斷地付出，並且從不要求任何回報。</u> This kind of love can be found in the story of "The Giving Tree". The tree loved a little boy, so she was happy to do everything for the boy. She gave her leaves to the boy to make into crowns when he was young and wanted to play the king. She let him sleep in her shade when he was tired. And she also let him climb up her trunk and swing from her branches when he was older. When he was mature enough to ask for money, she gave him her apples so that the boy could make money by selling them. When he became an adult, <u>2.她讓他砍下她的樹枝去蓋自己的房子，並且砍倒她的樹幹去做船。</u> Do you think it fair that a child merely takes and takes while a mother always gives and gives like the Giving Tree?

1. ....

2. ....

TEST 23 詳解

1. *Mothers just continuingly give, never asking anything for*
   return.【誤】

   * 須將 continuingly 改成 continuously (不斷地)，且 for 須改成 in。

   → A mother just $\left\{ \begin{array}{l} \text{keeps giving and giving,} \\ \text{gives continuously,} \end{array} \right\}$

   and she never $\left\{ \begin{array}{l} \text{asks for anything in return.} \\ \text{expects any repayment.} \end{array} \right.$ 【正】

2. *she let him cut down her branches to build his house and cut*
   down her trunk to make a boat.【誤】

   * 「砍下」是 cut off，故須將 cut down her branches 改成 cut off
   her branches。

   → she $\left\{ \begin{array}{l} \text{let him} \\ \text{allowed him to} \end{array} \right\}$ cut off her branches to build his

   own house and cut down her trunk to $\left\{ \begin{array}{l} \text{make} \\ \text{build} \end{array} \right\}$ a boat. 【正】

【註釋】 unconditional〔͵ʌnkən'dɪʃən̩〕adj. 無條件的
   selfless〔'sɛlflɪs〕adj. 無私的
   leaves〔livz〕n. pl. 葉子【單數是 leaf】
   crown〔kraʊn〕n. 皇冠   play〔ple〕v. 扮演
   shade〔ʃed〕n. 樹蔭   trunk〔trʌŋk〕n. 樹幹
   swing〔swɪŋ〕v. 懸吊於 <from>
   branch〔bræntʃ〕n. 樹枝   mature〔mə'tʃʊr〕adj. 成熟的
   fair〔fɛr〕adj. 公平的   merely〔'mɪrlɪ〕adv. 只是
   in return 作為回報   *cut off* 砍斷   *cut down* 砍倒

TEST 24

說明：下面一段短文中，有數處係以中文呈現，請利用上下文線索（如單字、片語等）將其譯成正確、通順、達意且前後連貫的英文。

Some students in senior high school find it difficult to deal with their heavy schoolwork. They feel overloaded. Although most of what they do day and night is study, they can never get all their work done. 1.挫折與沮喪使他們對學校課業失去興趣。 They may refuse to study. However, it is wrong to have such a negative attitude at this point. Magnificent achievements can come from desperate or seemingly hopeless conditions. 2.如果學生可以下定決心面對挑戰而不是放棄， they will find learning is not that difficult at all. Soon they will enjoy the fruit of success.

1. ....

2. ....

TEST 24 詳解

1. *The frustration and depression make them lose interest in school course.*【誤】（中正高中 孟耿德同學）

 * course 為可數名詞，故須改成 courses。

 → Frustration and depression cause them to lose interest in their school lessons. 【正】

2. *If students could be determine to face challenge instead of giving up,*【誤】（中正高中 孟耿德同學）

 * determine 須改為 determined，be determined to V.「決心要…」
 (= *determine to V.*)。

 → If students can $\begin{Bmatrix} \text{resolve} \\ \text{determine} \end{Bmatrix}$ to face the challenge $\begin{cases} \text{instead of giving up,} \\ \text{rather than give up,} \end{cases}$ 【正】

【註釋】 ***deal with*** 應付；處理　　schoolwork (ˈskulˌwɜk) *n.* 學業
overloaded (ˈovɚˈlodɪd) *adj.* 負擔過重的
get sth. done 將某事做完　　refuse (rɪˈfjuz) *v.* 拒絕
negative (ˈnɛgətɪv) *adj.* 負面的；否定的
at this point 在這時候
magnificent (mægˈnɪfəsn̩t) *adj.* 壯麗的；很棒的
achievements (əˈtʃivmənts) *n. pl.* 成就
desperate (ˈdɛspərɪt) *adj.* 無望的；絕望的
seemingly (ˈsimɪŋlɪ) *adv.* 似乎　　fruit (frut) *n.* 成果
frustration (frʌsˈtreʃən) *n.* 挫折
depression (dɪˈprɛʃən) *n.* 沮喪　　resolve (rɪˈzalv) *v.* 決心
determine (dɪˈtɜmɪn) *v.* 決心　　challenge (ˈtʃælɪndʒ) *n.* 挑戰
instead of 而不是　　***rather than*** 而不是

TEST 25

Children are taught how to live and how to act from the time they are born. It seems that they just play when they are four or five years old and in kindergarten. In fact, they are learning some important things. For example, 1.當他們學會不要打別人時，他們就是在學如何與別人相處。 When they are taught to clean up their own mess, they are being told to take responsibility for their own behavior. As for the habits of flushing after using the toilet and washing their hands before eating, 2.都在教他們衛生的重要。 These habits become second nature, so it is important for children to develop good habits in kindergarten. These will help them be happy and healthy long after they grow up.

1. ....

2. ....

TEST 25 詳解

1. *when they learn to not to hit others, they are learning how to*
   get along with them. 【誤】（陽明高中 馬筠同學）

   * learn to not to 須改爲 learn not to。

   → when they learn not to $\begin{Bmatrix} \text{hit} \\ \text{strike} \end{Bmatrix}$ others,

   they $\begin{Bmatrix} \text{are learning} \\ \text{learn} \end{Bmatrix}$ how to $\begin{Bmatrix} \text{get along with} \\ \text{live harmoniously with} \end{Bmatrix}$

   $\begin{Bmatrix} \text{others.} \\ \text{other people.} \end{Bmatrix}$ 【正】

2. *these are teaching them the importance of their sanitation.* 【誤】

   （陽明高中 馬筠同學）

   * 須將 their 去掉。

   → $\begin{Bmatrix} \text{these} \\ \text{they} \end{Bmatrix}$ teach them $\begin{Bmatrix} \text{the importance of hygiene.} \\ \text{how important cleanliness is.} \end{Bmatrix}$ 【正】

【註釋】　act〔ækt〕v. 採取行動
　　　　　kindergarten〔'kɪndɚ͵gɑrtn̩〕n. 幼稚園
　　　　　clean up 將～清理乾淨　　mess〔mɛs〕n. 雜亂
　　　　　take responsibility 負責任　　***as for*** 至於
　　　　　flush〔flʌʃ〕v. 沖水　　toilet〔'tɔɪlɪt〕n. 馬桶
　　　　　second nature 第二天性；習慣　　develop〔dɪ'vɛləp〕v. 培養
　　　　　grow up 長大　　***get along with*** 與～相處
　　　　　harmoniously〔hɑr'monɪəslɪ〕adv. 和諧地
　　　　　hygiene〔'haɪdʒin〕n. 衛生
　　　　　cleanliness〔'klɛnlɪnɪs〕n. 清潔；愛乾淨
　　　　　sanitation〔͵sænə'teʃən〕n. 衛生

TEST 26

When I was 21 years old, a wise man gave me the advice that one may give away everything, including money, besides one's heart. He told me that once the heart is given away, what one will get in return will be plenty of sighs and regret. However, 1. 因為我當時太年輕而且天真，我對他的忠告充耳不聞。 I soon had a crush on one of my classmates, who was handsome and athletic, but he turned me down. Not until then did I realize the importance of keeping one's fancy free. By the time I was 22, 2. 失戀痛苦的 經驗使我成熟很多。 If time could go back, I would take the advice of that wise man at 21.

1. ....

2. ....

TEST 26 詳解

1. *because I was so young and simple at that time, I was ignorant with his advice.*【誤】（大同高中 陳樺彬同學）

   * was ignorant with 須改為 ignored（忽視）或 turned a deaf ear to（對…充耳不聞）。

   → because I was too young and $\left\{\begin{array}{l}\text{innocent}\\\text{naive}\end{array}\right\}$ then,

   I turned a deaf ear to his advice. 【正】

2. *the experience of the agony of falling out of love makes me mature a lot.*【誤】（大同高中 陳樺彬同學）

   * 須將 the experience of the agony of 改成 the bitter experience of，而依句意為過去完成式，故 makes 須改為 had made。

   → the $\left\{\begin{array}{l}\text{bitter}\\\text{hard}\end{array}\right\}$ experience of $\left\{\begin{array}{l}\text{falling out of love}\\\text{failing at love}\end{array}\right\}$

   had matured me a lot. 【正】

【註釋】 advice〔əd'vaɪs〕n. 忠告；勸告　　*give away* 贈送
besides〔bɪ'saɪdz〕prep. 除了…之外（還有）
in return 作為回報　　sigh〔saɪ〕n. 嘆息
regret〔rɪ'grɛt〕n. 後悔　　*have a crush on* 迷戀
athletic〔æθ'lɛtɪk〕adj. 似運動選手的
turn down 拒絕　　fancy〔'fænsɪ〕n. 喜愛
keep one's *fancy free* 無戀愛對象；自由自在
take〔tek〕v. 聽從　　innocent〔'ɪnəsn̩t〕adj. 天真的
naive〔nɑ'iv〕adj. 天真的　　*turn a deaf ear to* 對～充耳不聞
fall out of love 失戀　　mature〔mə'tʃur〕v. 成熟

TEST 27

Foods higher in fat provide calories but few nutrients. 1. 在我們的飲食中，選擇較低脂的食物，並增加穀類產品、水果及蔬菜的量 are two things health experts have instructed people to do. However, a new study shows that a low-fat diet does not reduce our risk of getting cancer or heart disease. In the study, 2. 將近五萬名 50 至 79 歲的婦女，被要求要吃低脂的飲食。 They turned out to be no healthier than those who ate whatever they wanted.

1. ....

2. ....

TEST 27 詳解

1. *In our diet, choosing lower-fat food and increasing the capacity of grain products, fruits and vegetables* 【誤】（北一女中 陳柏玉同學）

* 須將 capacity（容量）改成 amount（數量），且將 in our diet 移至最後，並將 choosing 改成 Choosing。

$$\rightarrow \left.\begin{array}{l}\text{Choosing}\\\text{Selecting}\end{array}\right\}\left.\begin{array}{l}\text{lower-fat food}\\\text{food that is less fatty}\end{array}\right\}\text{ and}$$

$$\left\{\begin{array}{l}\text{increasing the amount of grain products, fruits,}\\\text{eating more grain products, fruits and}\end{array}\right.$$

$$\left.\begin{array}{l}\text{and vegetables in our diets}\\\text{vegetables}\end{array}\right\}\text{ 【正】}$$

2. *near 50 thousand of 50-79 years old women are asked to eat a low-fat diet.* 【誤】（北一女中 陳柏玉同學）

* 須將 50 thousand 改成 fifty thousand；50-79 years old 須改爲 50- to 79-year-old；依句意爲過去式，故 are 須改成 were。

$$\rightarrow \left.\begin{array}{l}\text{nearly}\\\text{almost}\end{array}\right\}\text{ 50,000 women}\left\{\begin{array}{l}\text{aged 50 to 79}\\\text{between the ages of 50 and 79}\end{array}\right.$$

$$\text{were asked to}\left\{\begin{array}{l}\text{eat}\\\text{follow}\end{array}\right\}\text{ a low-fat diet. 【正】}$$

【註釋】 **high in** 富含（= *rich in*）   calorie（ˈkælərɪ）*n.* 卡路里
nutrient（ˈnjutrɪənt）*n.* 營養素   instruct（ɪnˈstrʌkt）*v.* 教導
study（ˈstʌdɪ）*n.* 研究   ***turn out to be*** 結果是
fatty（ˈfætɪ）*adj.* 脂肪過多的；油膩的   grain（gren）*n.* 穀類
aged ~ ~歲的   follow（ˈfalo）*v.* 遵照

TEST 28

The number of languages in the world is way beyond your imagination. Of all the languages, English is the most widely spoken language in the history of our planet. As a matter of fact, 1. 英語幾乎在我們的生活的每一方面都扮演非常重要的角色。 Half of the world's books are written in English and most international phone calls are made in English. 2. 超過百分之七十的國際郵件都是用英文寫的。 In addition, English has the most words of all the world's languages. English is a crazy language because there are too many irregularities. However, it is the irregularities that make English interesting.

1. ....

2. ....

TEST 28 詳解

1. *English almost plays an important role on every side in our life.*【誤】（北一女中 林柔言同學）

   * 須將前面的 almost 去掉，並將 on every side in our life 改為 in almost every aspect of our lives。

   → English plays a very important $\begin{Bmatrix} \text{role} \\ \text{part} \end{Bmatrix}$ in $\begin{Bmatrix} \text{almost} \\ \text{nearly} \end{Bmatrix}$

   every $\begin{Bmatrix} \text{aspect} \\ \text{area} \end{Bmatrix}$ of our lives.【正】

2. *More than 70% national mails are written by English.*【誤】

   （北一女中 林柔言同學）

   * national（全國的）應改成 international（國際的），因為 mail 為不可數名詞，故 70% national mails are 須改成 70% of international mail is；又「用」英文寫，介系詞須用 in。

   → More than seventy percent of international mail

   is $\begin{cases} \text{written in English.} \\ \text{in English.} \end{cases}$【正】

【註釋】 *beyond one's imagination* 超乎某人的想像

planet（'plænɪt）*n.* 行星；地球

as a matter of fact 事實上　　*make a phone call* 打電話

in addition 此外　　crazy（'krezɪ）*adj.* 瘋狂的；奇怪的

irregularity（ɪˌrɛgjə'lærətɪ）*n.* 不規則

play（ple）*v.* 扮演　　role（rol）*n.* 角色

aspect（'æspɛkt）*n.* 方面　　mail（mel）*n.* 郵件

TEST 29

In time-conscious countries, where life is usually
fast-paced and hurried, 1.對人們而言，有效率地處理事情是
非常重要的。 Therefore, they expect themselves and
others to be punctual. In such places as North America
and Northern Europe, it is best to arrive right on time to
meetings and social engagements. If people do not, they
may insult their hosts and bosses. On the other hand,
many countries in South America, Africa, and the Middle
East have a more easygoing attitude toward time. In
these places, being on time is not always that necessary.
2.那裡的人寧願在街上和朋友聊天，也不願趕去參加辦公室會議。
For them, spending time with friends and family is far
more important than getting things done on time.

1. ....

2. ....

TEST 29 詳解

1. *it's important to deal with things effectively for people.* 【誤】

（景美女中 李家萱同學）

* important 前面須加 very；effectively（有效地）應改成 efficiently（有效率地）；須將 for people 移至 important 後面。

→ it's $\left\{\begin{array}{l}\text{of great importance} \\ \text{very important}\end{array}\right\}$ for people to $\left\{\begin{array}{l}\text{handle} \\ \text{deal with}\end{array}\right\}$

things efficiently. 【正】

2. *People there would rather chat with friends on the street than attend the office conference.* 【誤】 （景美女中 李家萱同學）

* attend 前面須加 hurry to（趕去）；「參加辦公室會議」是 attend the office meeting，attend the conference 則是「參加會議」，但不可說成 *attend the office conference*（誤）。

→ People there $\left\{\begin{array}{l}\text{would rather chat with friends on the} \\ \text{prefer chatting with friends on the}\end{array}\right.$

$\left.\begin{array}{l}\text{street than hurry to} \\ \text{street to rushing to}\end{array}\right\}$ $\left\{\begin{array}{l}\text{an office meeting.} \\ \text{a meeting at their office.}\end{array}\right.$ 【正】

【註釋】 time-conscious (ˈtaɪmˈkɑnʃəs) *adj.* 注重時間觀念的
　　　　 fast-paced (ˈfæstˈpest) *adj.* 步調快的
　　　　 hurried (ˈhɜɪd) *adj.* 匆忙的　　 punctual (ˈpʌŋktʃuəl) *adj.* 準時的
　　　　 right on time 正好準時　　 *social engagement* 社交聚會
　　　　 insult (ɪnˈsʌlt) *v.* 侮辱　　 easygoing (ˈizɪˈgoɪŋ) *adj.* 悠哉的
　　　　 of importance 重要的 (= *important*)
　　　　 handle (ˈhændl̩) *v.* 處理 (= *deal with*)
　　　　 efficiently (əˈfɪʃəntlɪ) *adv.* 有效率地
　　　　 would rather V₁ than V₂ 寧願 V₁ 也不願 V₂ (= *prefer V-ing₁ to V-ing₂*)　　 chat (tʃæt) *v.* 聊天　　 *hurry to* 趕去 (= *rush to*)

TEST 30

Even though continued study has shown that cloud seeding can have an effect on the weather, we still have not come very far in learning how to control the weather. 1. 但是我們對於造成天氣的因素及如何預測天氣的了解 has increased by leaps and bounds. Weather affects every aspect of our lives. Even if we cannot control it, 2. 了解和預測它能幫助我們減少它對我們的影響。 And that increases control of our lives.

1. ....

2. ....

TEST 30 詳解

1. *But our understand for the factor of weather and how to predict weather*【誤】（景美女中 楊鈺涵同學）

    * 須將動詞 understand 改成動名詞 understanding 或名詞 knowledge（了解），且 for the factor of 須改為 of the factors of。

    → But our knowledge of $\begin{cases} \text{what causes} \\ \text{the causes of} \end{cases}$ weather

    and of how to $\begin{cases} \text{predict} \\ \text{forecast} \end{cases}$ weather【正】

2. *understanding and predicting it can help us decrease the effect by it.*【誤】（景美女中 楊鈺涵同學）

    * the effect by it 須改為 its effect on us（它對我們的影響）。

    → understanding and predicting it helps us $\begin{cases} \text{lessen} \\ \text{reduce} \end{cases}$

    $\begin{cases} \text{its effect on us.} \\ \text{the effect it has on us.} \end{cases}$【正】

【註釋】 continued〔kən'tɪnjʊd〕*adj.* 持續不斷的
　　　　 cloud seeding 種雲　　effect〔ɪ'fɛkt〕*n.* 影響
　　　　 come far 大有進展
　　　　 by leaps and bounds 非常迅速地
　　　　 affect〔ə'fɛkt〕*v.* 影響　　aspect〔'æspɛkt〕*n.* 方面
　　　　 predict〔prɪ'dɪkt〕*v.* 預測
　　　　 forecast〔for'kæst〕*v.* 預測　　lessen〔'lɛsn̩〕*v.* 減少

TEST 31

Thomas is a college student 1. 他最喜歡的消遣就是在電影院看最新的影片。 Though he's low on money, he can't resist going to the movie theaters. Ellen, Thomas' friend, has come up with a solution for him, 2. 那就是他可以從網路上免費下載最新的電影。 Knowing it is illegal to download movies from the Internet, Thomas would prefer to split the cost of DVDs with his roommate, Charles, than to steal the films from the Internet.

1. ....

2. ....

TEST 31 詳解

1. *His favorite entertainment is watching the newest film in theater.*【誤】(薇閣高中 李冠瑢同學)

* 本句為不完整句，故 His 須改成 whose；in theater 須改為 in the theater 或 at the theater。

→ whose $\begin{cases} \text{favorite} \\ \text{preferred} \end{cases}$ pastime is $\begin{cases} \text{watching} \\ \text{seeing} \end{cases}$

the latest movies $\begin{cases} \text{in the movie theaters.} \\ \text{at the cinema.} \end{cases}$ 【正】

2. *which is that he can download the newest film through Internet.*【誤】(薇閣高中 李冠瑢同學)

* film through Internet 須改成 film for free from the Internet。

→ which is that he can $\begin{cases} \text{download the latest movies} \\ \text{use the Internet to download} \end{cases}$

for free from the Internet.
new movies without paying for them. $\Big\}$ 【正】

【註釋】 low〔lo〕adj. 不夠的；缺乏的　　resist〔rɪ'zɪst〕v. 抗拒
　　　　come up with 想出　　solution〔sə'luʃən〕n. 解決之道
　　　　illegal〔ɪ'ligḷ〕adj. 非法的　　download〔'daʊn,lod〕v. 下載
　　　　Internet〔'ɪntɚ,nɛt〕n. 網際網路　　**split the cost** 分攤費用
　　　　roommate〔'rum,met〕n. 室友
　　　　film〔fɪlm〕n. 影片 (= movie)
　　　　pastime〔'pæs,taɪm〕n. 消遣
　　　　latest〔'letɪst〕adj. 最新的 (= newest)
　　　　cinema〔'sɪnəmə〕n. 電影院 (= theater)　　**for free** 免費地

TEST 32

Marketing specialists have worked out some strategies to make us buy more in their supermarkets. One of the commonly used methods is to place items in a special way so we will buy more. For example, simple, ordinary food is placed in different sections so we have to walk by more aisles to find what we need. More expensive items are put in packages with bright colors and pictures 1. 並且放在眼睛容易看到的高度，這樣我們就能立刻看到它們，並且想要買它們。

In addition, they make the supermarkets as pleasant as they can with comfortable temperatures in summer and winter and soft music playing all the time. If we stay there long enough, they are able to get more money out of our pockets. 2. 每星期超市也會以較低或特別的價格，來賣一些東西 to promote certain products. If we don't want to spend more money than necessary in a supermarket, we must be careful of the tricks marketing specialists are trying to play on us.

1. ....

2. ....

TEST 32 詳解

1. <u>at the height of eye level so that we can see them right away</u> <u>and want to buy them.</u>【誤】（中山女中 蘇郁雯同學）

   * at the height of eye level 須改成 and placed at eye level；而 and want to 須改成 and will want to。

   $$\rightarrow \text{and} \begin{Bmatrix} \text{placed} \\ \text{put} \end{Bmatrix} \text{at} \begin{Bmatrix} \text{eye level} \\ \text{the height of our eyes} \end{Bmatrix} \begin{Bmatrix} \text{so} \\ \text{so that} \end{Bmatrix} \text{we can}$$

   $$\text{see them} \begin{Bmatrix} \text{right away} \\ \text{immediately} \end{Bmatrix} \text{and will want to} \begin{Bmatrix} \text{buy} \\ \text{purchase} \end{Bmatrix}$$

   them. 【正】

2. <u>The supermarkets every week also sell some stuffs at a lower</u> <u>or special price</u>【誤】（中山女中 蘇郁雯同學）

   * 須將 every week 移至句尾；stuff 爲不可數名詞，須將 stuffs 改爲 things。

   $$\rightarrow \text{Supermarkets also sell} \begin{Bmatrix} \text{some} \\ \text{certain} \end{Bmatrix} \text{things at} \begin{Bmatrix} \text{lower} \\ \text{reduced} \end{Bmatrix},$$

   or special, prices every week 【正】

【註釋】 ***marketing specialist*** 行銷專家　　***work out*** 想出
strategy〔'strætədʒɪ〕*n.* 策略　　commonly〔'kɑmənlɪ〕*adv.* 通常
place〔ples〕*v.* 放置　　item〔'aɪtəm〕*n.* 物品
ordinary〔'ɔrdn̩͵ɛrɪ〕*adj.* 普通的　　section〔'sɛkʃən〕*n.* 區域
aisle〔aɪl〕*n.* 走道　　package〔'pækɪdʒ〕*n.* 包裝
in addition 此外　　pleasant〔'plɛznt〕*adj.* 令人愉快的
as…as *one can* 儘可能　　play〔ple〕*v.* 播放
pocket〔'pɑkɪt〕*n.* 口袋　　promote〔prə'mot〕*v.* 促銷
certain〔'sɝtn̩〕*adj.* 某些　　***play a trick on*** *sb.* 欺騙某人
eye level 眼睛的高度　　***reduced price*** 折扣價格

TEST 33

説明：下面一段短文中，有數處係以中文呈現，請利用上下文線索（如單字、片語等）將其譯成正確、通順、達意且前後連貫的英文。

Grandpa loves to recount the story of his first date with Grandma. 1. <u>在她知道他的存在以前，他就已經迷戀她了。</u> Grandma was so beautiful that dozens of guys waited in line in front of her house every day just to talk to her. Being of a shy nature, Grandpa thought about giving up. 2. <u>然而，就在那特別的一天，他的命運完全扭轉了。</u> On his way home from school, he saw a bunch of bullies making fun of Grandma. His first reaction was to rescue her. He was unbelievably brave and showed what he had learned in karate class. When Grandma said thanks to him, he had butterflies in his stomach and even couldn't breathe!

1. ....

2. ....

TEST 33　詳解

1. *He had fallen in love with her before she know him.* 【誤】

（成功高中 呂友文同學）

　　* know 須改成過去式動詞 knew，但句意是「知道他的存在」，故應改成 learned of his existence。

$$\rightarrow \text{He} \begin{Bmatrix} \text{had had a crush on} \\ \text{was in love with} \end{Bmatrix} \text{her before she learned}$$

　　of his existence. 【正】

2. *However, on the special day, his fate was completely changed.* 【誤】（成功高中 呂友文同學）

　　* changed（改變）須改成 reversed（扭轉）。

$$\rightarrow \text{However, on that special day, his} \begin{Bmatrix} \text{fate} \\ \text{luck} \end{Bmatrix} \text{was}$$

　　completely reversed. 【正】

【註釋】　recount〔rɪ'kaʊnt〕v. 詳述；細說　　date〔det〕n. 約會
　　　　　dozens of 數十個　　guy〔gaɪ〕n. 男人；傢伙
　　　　　wait in line 排隊等候　　shy〔ʃaɪ〕adj. 害羞的
　　　　　nature〔'netʃɚ〕n. 本性　　***give up*** 放棄
　　　　　a bunch of 一群　　bully〔'bʊlɪ〕n. 惡霸
　　　　　make fun of 嘲弄；取笑　　reaction〔rɪ'ækʃən〕n. 反應
　　　　　unbelievably〔ˌʌnbɪ'livəblɪ〕adv. 不可思議地
　　　　　brave〔brev〕adj. 勇敢的　　karate〔kə'rɑtɪ〕n. 空手道
　　　　　say thanks to 向～道謝
　　　　　have butterflies in one's ***stomach*** 忐忑不安
　　　　　breathe〔brið〕v. 呼吸　　***have a crush on*** 迷戀
　　　　　learn of 得知　　existence〔ɪg'zɪstəns〕n. 存在
　　　　　fate〔fet〕n. 命運　　reverse〔rɪ'vɝs〕v. 逆轉

TEST 34

Percy Shaw, the inventor of the "cat's-eye" reflector, came up with the good idea when driving along a winding road one night. Shaw knew the road well, but suddenly, just before a turn, he ran into thick fog. He could see almost nothing ahead 1.而且甚至無法判斷他離邊緣有多遠。 Strangely enough, in the dark, two small points of light shone through the fog. They were his own headlights, reflected in the eyes of a cat. 2.他開始研發會像貓眼般發亮的反光裝置。 And his invention has made roads safe to drive along after dark.

1. ....

2. ....

TEST 34 詳解

1. *and even cannot judge how far he was from the edge.* 【誤】

（北一女中 黃韻儒同學）

* cannot 須改成過去式的 could not。

$$\rightarrow \text{and} \left\{ \begin{array}{l} \text{even could not tell} \\ \text{he didn't even know} \end{array} \right\} \text{how far}$$

$$\left\{ \begin{array}{l} \text{he was from the edge.} \\ \text{away the edge was.} \end{array} \right. 【正】$$

2. *He started to invent reflection device which sparkles like cat's eyes.* 【誤】（北一女中 黃韻儒同學）

* invent reflection device 須改成 develop a reflective device；
而 cat's eyes 須改為 a cat's eyes，或 cats' eyes。

$$\rightarrow \text{He began to develop reflectors that} \left\{ \begin{array}{l} \text{shine} \\ \text{give off light} \end{array} \right\}$$

$$\left\{ \begin{array}{l} \text{like a cat's eyes.} \\ \text{just as a cat's eyes do.} \end{array} \right. 【正】$$

【註釋】 inventor (ɪnˈvɛntɚ) *n.* 發明者
reflector (rɪˈflɛktɚ) *n.* 反光裝置 *come up with* 想出
winding (ˈwaɪndɪŋ) *adj.* 蜿蜒的
suddenly (ˈsʌdn̩lɪ) *adv.* 突然地 turn (tɜn) *n.* 轉彎
run into 撞上；碰上 *thick fog* 濃霧
strangely enough 奇怪的是 shine (ʃaɪn) *v.* 發光；閃爍
headlight (ˈhɛd.laɪt) *n.* 頭燈；大燈
reflect (rɪˈflɛkt) *v.* 反射 *after dark* 天黑以後
edge (ɛdʒ) *n.* 邊緣 develop (dɪˈvɛləp) *v.* 研發

TEST 35

One night when I was about to go to bed, I felt the house shaking violently. At the same time, Lucky, my pet puppy, would not stop barking. Most of the books on the shelf fell down onto the floor. The chicks in the backyard ran up and down. At that time, 1. 我除了躲在桌子下，雙眼緊閉之外，什麼也不能做。 I was scared to death. Minutes later, I heard on the radio that Taiwan had been hit by the worst earthquake in one hundred years, which measured 7.3 on the Richter Scale. In this disaster, 2. 數千人死亡，而且有數十萬人無家可歸。

1. ....

2. ....

TEST 35 詳解

1. *I can't do nothing but stay under the table closing my eyes.* 【誤】

（北一女中 江欣璇同學）

* nothing 須改成 anything，且 stay 應改成 hide（躲藏），而 closing my eyes 須改成 and close my eyes。

→ $\left\{\begin{array}{l}\text{I could do nothing but} \\ \text{there was nothing I could do except}\end{array}\right\}$ hide under

the table $\left\{\begin{array}{l}\text{, with my eyes closed.} \\ \text{and close my eyes.}\end{array}\right.$ 【正】

2. *thousands of people died and hundreds of thousands of people become homeless.* 【誤】 （北一女中 江欣璇同學）

* 依句意為過去式，故 become 須改為 became。

→ thousands of people $\left\{\begin{array}{l}\text{were killed} \\ \text{died}\end{array}\right\}$ and hundreds

of thousands of people $\left\{\begin{array}{l}\text{became homeless.} \\ \text{lost their homes.}\end{array}\right.$ 【正】

【註釋】　violently (ˈvaɪələntlɪ) adv. 劇烈地　　pet (pɛt) adj. 寵物的
puppy (ˈpʌpɪ) n. 小狗　　shelf (ʃɛlf) n. 架子
chick (tʃɪk) n. 小雞　　backyard (ˈbækˈjɑrd) n. 後院
up and down 到處　　*be scared to death* 嚇得半死
hit (hɪt) v. 侵襲　　worst (wɜst) adj. 最嚴重的
measure (ˈmɛʒɚ) v. (強度) 有…
the Richter Scale 芮氏地震儀　　disaster (dɪzˈæstɚ) n. 災難
can do nothing but V. 只能… (= have nothing to do but/except V.)
be killed 死亡　　*hundreds of thousands of* 數十萬的
homeless (ˈhomlɪs) adj. 無家可歸的

TEST 36

> 說明：下面一段短文中，有數處係以中文呈現，請利用上下
> 文線索（如單字、片語等）將其譯成正確、通順、達
> 意且前後連貫的英文。

　　Susan, my best friend, seems to have a problem with germs and mess. For example, she cleans her house seven days a week. Whenever she cleans, she uses hot water and soap to wash every part of the floor 1.為了使地板發亮，以及殺死病菌。 In addition, she can't stand sharing space with messy things, 2.所以她總是立刻把她的東西收拾整齊。 I have told her not to clean the house like this; however, she seems to enjoy doing it.

1. ....

2. ....

TEST 36 詳解

1. *in order to shine the floor and kill the bacteria.*【誤】

　　* 須將 bacteria (細菌) 改爲 germs (病菌)。

　→ in order to shine the floor as well as to kill germs.【正】

　或 for the purpose of shining the floor and killing

　　germs.【正】

2. *as a result, she always makes her things in orders immediately.*【誤】

　　* 須將 makes her things in orders 改成 puts her things in order。

　→ so she always puts $\left\{ \begin{array}{l} \text{her things away tidily} \\ \text{things in their proper place} \end{array} \right\}$

　$\left\{ \begin{array}{l} \text{immediately.} \\ \text{right away.} \end{array} \right.$【正】

【註釋】　germ〔dʒʒm〕*n.* 病菌

　　　　　mess〔mɛs〕*n.* 混亂；髒亂　　soap〔sop〕*n.* 肥皂

　　　　　in addition 此外　　stand〔stænd〕*v.* 忍受

　　　　　share〔ʃɛr〕*v.* 分享；共用

　　　　　messy〔'mɛsɪ〕*adj.* 雜亂的

　　　　　shine〔ʃaɪn〕*v.* 擦亮　　*as well as* 以及

　　　　　put away 收拾　　tidily〔'taɪdɪlɪ〕*adv.* 整潔地

　　　　　proper〔'prɑpɚ〕*adj.* 適當的

TEST 37

Problems like having too much stress from your studies or from your parents, not being popular with your classmates and not having enough time may make you unhappy as a high school freshman. Grumbling or complaining, however, can provide you no help. Besides, you are not alone. Every freshman has the same worries that you do. 1. 你所必須做的，就是用積極的方式來處置它們，such as making a deal with your parents for more free time, making friends with some classmates first and setting a workable time schedule. 2. 如果你聽從上面的忠告，並把它付諸行動，you will be surprised at how much you may change in your life.

1. ....

2. ....

TEST 37 詳解

1. *What you have to do is that using positive way to deal with them,* 【誤】（南湖高中 陳映儒同學）

   * What 須改成 All；all you have to do is + V.「你所必須做的就是…」，故 that using…them，須改成 deal with them in a positive way。

   → All you have to do is $\left\{\begin{array}{l}\text{deal with}\\\text{handle}\end{array}\right\}$ them in a positive way, 【正】

2. *If you follow the above advices and carry out them,* 【誤】

   （南湖高中 陳映儒同學）

   * advice 為不可數名詞，故 advices 須改成 advice；carry out them 須改成 carry it out。

   → If you take the above advice and put it into action, 【正】

【註釋】　stress〔strɛs〕*n.* 壓力　　studies〔'stʌdɪz〕*n. pl.* 學業

　　　　　be popular with 受～歡迎

　　　　　freshman〔'frɛʃmən〕*n.* 高一新生；大一新鮮人

　　　　　grumble〔'grʌmbl̩〕*v.* 抱怨

　　　　　complain〔kəm'plen〕*v.* 抱怨　　alone〔ə'lon〕*adj.* 孤單的

　　　　　make a deal with *sb.* 和某人達成協議

　　　　　free time 空閒時間　　set〔sɛt〕*v.* 設定

　　　　　workable〔'wɜkəbl̩〕*adj.* 行得通的

　　　　　schedule〔'skɛdʒul〕*n.* 時間表

　　　　　All *one* ***has to do is*** *V.* 某人所必須做的就是…

　　　　　deal with 處置　　positive〔'pazətɪv〕*adj.* 正面的；積極的

　　　　　take〔tek〕*v.* 聽從　　***put～into action*** 將～付諸行動

TEST 38

Living in a modern, high technology world, we all should be aware of the fact that science plays a big role in the kitchen. If you can put all the science you learn in school to good use, cooking will become much easier and more efficient. For example, 1. 或許你不知道水煮蛋為何總是在熱水中裂開。 That's an easy physics lesson: heated air expands! So, how can you avoid this? As you know, there is a small air bubble at the fat end of an egg. 2. 用一根大頭針在蛋較胖的那一端刺個小洞 before you boil it. This will give the expanding air a way to escape without cracking the shell. And then, you will have beautiful, unbroken eggs in your dish.

1. ....

2. ....

TEST 38 詳解

1. *maybe you didn't know why boiled-eggs always crack in hot water.*【誤】（西松高中 梁翔同學）

* 依句意為現在式，故 didn't 須改為 don't；「水煮蛋」是 boiled eggs。

→ $\left\{ \begin{array}{l} \text{perhaps} \\ \text{maybe} \end{array} \right\}$ you don't know why boiled eggs always

$\left\{ \begin{array}{l} \text{split} \\ \text{crack} \end{array} \right\}$ open in hot water.【正】

2. *Using a pin…a small hole on the fatter side of eggs*【誤】

（西松高中 梁翔同學）

* 依句意為祈使句，故句首用原形動詞 Use，寫成：Use a pin and make a small hole；on 須改成 in，且句尾的 eggs 須改成 the egg。

→ Use a pin $\left\{ \begin{array}{l} \text{to} \\ \text{and} \end{array} \right\}$ make a small hole in the fat

end of the egg【正】

【註釋】 technology〔tɛk'nɑlədʒɪ〕 *n.* 科技
be aware of 知道
play a big role 扮演一個重要的角色
put ~ to use 利用~　efficient〔ə'fɪʃənt〕 *adj.* 有效率的
physics〔'fɪzɪks〕 *n.* 物理學　heated〔'hitɪd〕 *adj.* 加熱的
expand〔ɪk'spænd〕 *v.* 膨脹　bubble〔'bʌbḷ〕 *n.* 泡泡
crack〔kræk〕 *v.* 使破裂　shell〔ʃɛl〕 *n.* 殼
dish〔dɪʃ〕 *n.* 盤子；菜餚　boiled〔bɔɪld〕 *adj.* 煮熟的
split open 裂開　pin〔pɪn〕 *n.* 大頭針

TEST 39

Why do so many grownups forget the simple things of childhood? As time goes by, we become busier and busier at school and then at work. 1.而且逐漸地，我們就忘記以前玩得有多麼愉快。 We seldom think of what it feels like to swing on a swing, or to watch leaves blowing in the wind. We forget how wonderful it is to let our minds wander and imagine. 2.小孩的詩能幫助我們記得這些童年的快樂。 The fun, silly, imaginary things in the poems were once such a big part of our lives. Children's poetry is for anyone who knows how special it is to be and feel like a child. So, why not try to read it sometimes?

1. ....

2. ....

TEST 39 詳解

1. *And gradually forget how happy in the past.*【誤】（中正高中 張惟筑同學）

   * 「玩得愉快」是 have fun，故 how happy 須改成 how much fun we had。

   → And $\left\{\begin{array}{l}\text{gradually,} \\ \text{little by little,}\end{array}\right\}$ we forget

   $\left\{\begin{array}{l}\text{how much fun we used to have.} \\ \text{that we used to have a lot of fun.}\end{array}\right.$ 【正】

2. *The children's poem can help us remember the happiness of childhood.*【誤】（中正高中 張惟筑同學）

   * The children's poem 須改成 Children's poetry。

   → Children's poetry $\left\{\begin{array}{l}\text{can help} \\ \text{helps}\end{array}\right\}$ us $\left\{\begin{array}{l}\text{remember} \\ \text{recall}\end{array}\right\}$

   $\left\{\begin{array}{l}\text{these joys of childhood.} \\ \text{the pleasures of being a child.}\end{array}\right.$ 【正】

【註釋】 grownup (ˈgronˌʌp) n. 成人　　childhood (ˈtʃaɪldˌhʊd) n. 童年
as time goes by 隨著時間的過去　　*swing on a swing* 盪鞦韆
blow (blo) v. 吹　　wander (ˈwɑndɚ) v. 徘徊；流浪
imagine (ɪˈmædʒɪn) v. 想像
fun (fʌn) adj. 有趣的　　n. 樂趣　　silly (ˈsɪlɪ) adj. 愚蠢的
imaginary (ɪˈmædʒəˌnɛrɪ) adj. 虛構的　　poem (ˈpoˑɪm) n. 詩
once (wʌns) adv. 曾經　　poetry (ˈpoˑɪtrɪ) n. 詩【集合名詞】
gradually (ˈgrædʒʊəlɪ) adv. 逐漸地（= *little by little*）
in the past 以前　　*have fun* 玩得愉快　　*used to* 以前

TEST 40

說明：下面一段短文中，有數處係以中文呈現，請利用上下
　　　文線索（如單字、片語等）將其譯成正確、通順、達
　　　意且前後連貫的英文。

Linda and Gabe went to IIan to learn more about
how to plant green onions. First, farmers taught
them that they needed to plow the soil. <u>1. 然後，他們
在土壤上放乾草，使得雜草無法生長。</u> After that, they
split each green onion stem into two or three stems.
Finally, they could harvest the green onions. The
green onions needed to be washed. The farmers
washed and weighed them, and put them in storage.
<u>2. 它們被保存在一個特別的冰箱裡一段時間。</u> Then, the
green onions were sold at the market.

1. ....

2. ....

TEST 40 詳解

1. *Then, they put dried grass on the soil to keep bad grass not to grow.*【誤】(成淵高中 謝采芸同學)

   * *keep ~ from V-ing*「使~無法…」，故須將 not to grow 改成 from growing；bad grass 應改成 weeds (雜草)。

   → $\left.\begin{array}{l}\text{Then,}\\\text{Next,}\end{array}\right\}$ they put dry grass over the soil

   to $\left\{\begin{array}{l}\text{prevent}\\\text{keep}\end{array}\right\}$ weeds from $\left\{\begin{array}{l}\text{growing.}\\\text{sprouting.}\end{array}\right.$【正】

2. *They are preserved at a special refregirator for a period of time.*【誤】(成淵高中 謝采芸同學)

   * 須將 at 改成 in；refregirator 拼錯，須改成 refrigerator (冰箱)。

   → They were $\left\{\begin{array}{l}\text{kept}\\\text{stored}\end{array}\right\}$ in a special refrigerator

   for $\left\{\begin{array}{l}\text{some time.}\\\text{a while.}\end{array}\right.$【正】

【註釋】 plant〔plænt〕v. 種植　　onion〔'ʌnjən〕n. 洋蔥
plow〔plaʊ〕v. 犁　　soil〔sɔɪl〕n. 土壤
split〔splɪt〕v. 劈開；使分裂　　stem〔stɛm〕n. 莖
harvest〔'hɑrvɪst〕v. 收割；收穫　　weigh〔we〕v. 稱…的重量
storage〔'storɪdʒ〕n. 貯藏；倉庫
put ~ in storage 把~放入倉庫保管
market〔'mɑrkɪt〕n. 市場　　grass〔græs〕n. 草
keep…from 使…無法~　　weed〔wid〕n. 雜草
refrigerator〔rɪ'frɪdʒə,retə〕n. 冰箱

TEST　41

說明：下面一段短文中，有數處係以中文呈現，請利用上下文線索（如單字、片語等）將其譯成正確、通順、達意且前後連貫的英文。

　　Astrology is popular nowadays. Everyone has a star sign that corresponds to his or her birthday. Each sign belongs to one of the four categories: fire, earth, air and water. 1.火象星座的人通常充滿熱情，容易成為偉大的領導者。 As for those who are born under the air signs, they are eager for knowledge and often surround themselves with friends. How about people belonging to the earth category? They always follow the plans they make and are known for their strong wills. The last category is people born under the water signs. They like to follow the heart instead of the mind. 2.你可以在一些藝術家身上找到這個人格特質，他們通常非常有想像力，而且敏感。

1. ....

2. ....

TEST 41 詳解

1. *Those fire star sign usually filled with passion, easy to become an amazing leader.*【誤】（板橋高中 劉娟安同學）

   * Those fire star sign 須改為 Those of the fire star sign are；easy to 須改為 and tend to；an amazing leader 須改為 great leaders。

   $$\rightarrow \left\{ \begin{array}{l} \text{Fire-sign people} \\ \text{People born under the fire signs} \end{array} \right\} \text{are often}$$

   $$\left\{ \begin{array}{l} \text{full of passion} \\ \text{passionate} \end{array} \right\} \text{and} \left\{ \begin{array}{l} \text{tend to} \\ \text{have a tendency to} \end{array} \right\}$$

   become great leaders.【正】

2. *You can find those character in some of artists, they usually rich in imagination and sensible.*【誤】（板橋高中 劉娟安同學）

   * these character（人格）須改為 this personality trait（這個人格特質）；they usually rich 須改為 who are usually rich，且 sensible（明智的）須改為 sensitive（敏感的）。

   $$\rightarrow \text{You can find this personality trait in some artists, who}$$

   are usually $\left\{ \begin{array}{l} \text{very} \\ \text{highly} \end{array} \right\}$ imaginative and sensitive.【正】

【註釋】 astrology〔əˈstrɑlədʒɪ〕*n.* 占星術
   nowadays〔ˈnɑʊəˌdez〕*adv.* 現在 ***star sign*** 星座
   correspond to 符合 category〔ˈkætəˌgorɪ〕*n.* 範疇；類型
   earth〔ɝθ〕*n.* 泥土 eager〔ˈigɚ〕*adj.* 渴望的
   surround〔səˈraʊnd〕*v.* 使環繞 will〔wɪl〕*n.* 意志力
   instead of 而不是 passion〔ˈpæʃən〕*n.* 熱情
   tend to V. 易於… personality〔ˌpɝsṇˈælətɪ〕*n.* 人格
   trait〔tret〕*n.* 特質 highly〔ˈhaɪlɪ〕*adv.* 非常
   imaginative〔ɪˈmædʒəˌnetɪv〕*adj.* 有想像力的
   sensitive〔ˈsɛnsətɪv〕*adj.* 敏感的

TEST 42

Bette Nesmith Graham, a Dallas secretary and a single mother raising a son on her own, 1.是很受歡迎的文具立可白的發明人， which is used to cover up mistakes made on paper. Although she was an efficient employee, Graham still made typing errors when using an electric typewriter. Her work looked messy when she tried to erase her mistakes with a pencil eraser. As she watched holiday window painters remove dirty spots in their work, an idea began to grow in her mind. 2.何不像窗戶的油漆工一樣，掩飾打字的錯誤呢？ Graham used her own kitchen blender to mix up her first batch of Liquid Paper and turned a problem in her work into a good idea for an invention.

1. ....

2. ....

TEST 42 詳解

1. <u>*who is popular as the inventer of the correction pens,*</u>【誤】

* who is popular as 應改成 was；inventer 拼錯，應改成 inventor；而
the correction pens 應改為 the popular stationery Liquid Paper。

→ was the $\begin{cases} \text{inventor} \\ \text{creator} \end{cases}$ of $\begin{cases} \text{the popular stationery} \\ \text{Liquid Paper, a popular} \end{cases}$

Liquid Paper,
writing tool, $\Big\}$ 【正】

2. <u>*Why not be like the window painters, covering the mistakes*</u>
<u>*of typing?*</u>【誤】

* 應改成 Why not cover the typing mistakes…?

→ Why not cover up the typing mistakes

$\begin{cases} \text{as the window painters do?} \\ \text{in the same way that window painters do?} \end{cases}$ 【正】

【註釋】 ***single mother*** 單親媽媽　　raise〔rez〕*v.* 撫養
cover up 掩蓋　　efficient〔əˈfɪʃənt〕*adj.* 有效率的
employee〔ˌɛmplɔɪˈi〕*n.* 員工　　typing〔ˈtaɪpɪŋ〕*adj.* 打字的
error〔ˈɛrɚ〕*n.* 錯誤　　electric〔ɪˈlɛktrɪk〕*adj.* 電動的
typewriter〔ˈtaɪpˌraɪtɚ〕*n.* 打字機　　messy〔ˈmɛsɪ〕*adj.* 凌亂的
erase〔ɪˈres〕*v.* 擦掉；除去　　eraser〔ɪˈresɚ〕*n.* 橡皮擦
holiday〔ˈhɑləˌde〕*adj.* 假日的　　remove〔rɪˈmuv〕*v.* 除去
spot〔spɑt〕*n.* 點　　grow〔gro〕*v.* (逐漸) 形成
blender〔ˈblɛndɚ〕*n.* 攪拌器；果汁機　　***mix up*** 混合
batch〔bætʃ〕*n.* 一批；一團
Liquid Paper 立可白 (= *liquid paper*)
***turn* A *into* B** 把 A 變成 B　　inventor〔ɪnˈvɛntɚ〕*n.* 發明家
creator〔krɪˈetɚ〕*n.* 創造者　　stationery〔ˈsteʃənˌɛrɪ〕*n.* 文具

TEST 43

Studies show that pets can do people good. People with pets, especially dogs, seem to live longer than those without them. Besides, it has been discovered that petting a dog helps lower people's blood pressure. <u>1. 這就是為什麼有越來越多的狗已經接受訓練，成為治療犬</u> in recent years. Take Blackie for example. He is a much loved therapy dog that visits nursing homes. Once, Blackie saw an old lady who never spoke to others. He went up to her and wagged his tail as a greeting. <u>2. 令護士們驚訝的是，這位女士摸摸 Blackie 的頭，</u> and a smile began to brighten her face. As Blackie kept visiting her, she gradually turned into a smiling and energetic woman.

1. ....

2. ....

TEST 43 詳解

1. *That's why there are more and more dogs have been treated and becoming therapy dogs* 【誤】（景美女中 林品君同學）

  * 須將 there are 去掉；treated and becoming 須改為 trained to become。

  → This is why $\left\{ \begin{array}{l} \text{a growing} \\ \text{an increasing} \end{array} \right\}$ number of dogs have

  $\left\{ \begin{array}{l} \text{received training and become} \\ \text{been trained to be} \end{array} \right\}$ therapy dogs 【正】

2. *To the nursers surprise, the lady touched Blackie's head,* 【誤】

  （景美女中 林品君同學）

  * nursers 應改為 nurses'。

  → To the nurses' surprise, the lady petted Blackie's head, 【正】

【註釋】 pet〔pɛt〕n. 寵物　v. 撫摸

　　　　do sb. good 對某人有好處　　lower〔'loɚ〕v. 降低

　　　　blood pressure 血壓　　recent〔'risn̩t〕adj. 最近的

　　　　much loved 深受喜愛的　　therapy〔'θɛrəpɪ〕n. 治療

　　　　nursing home 療養院　　*go up to* 走近

　　　　wag〔wæg〕v. 搖擺　　greeting〔'gritɪŋ〕n. 打招呼

　　　　brighten〔'braɪtn̩〕v. 使發亮；使開朗

　　　　gradually〔'grædʒuəlɪ〕adv. 逐漸地

　　　　turn into 變成　　energetic〔ˌɛnɚ'dʒɛtɪk〕adj. 充滿活力的

　　　　growing〔'groɪŋ〕adj. 逐漸增加的

　　　　to one's surprise 令某人驚訝的是

TEST 44

説明：下面一段短文中，有數處係以中文呈現，請利用上下
文線索（如單字、片語等）將其譯成正確、通順、達
意且前後連貫的英文。

J. K. Rowling wrote her first book when she was six years old. Many years later, she started writing Harry Potter and the Philosopher's Stone while she was working as an English teacher in Portugal, 1.她在那裡結婚，後來又離婚。 After she left Portugal, she moved to Edinburgh, Scotland. 2.儘管身為單親媽媽生活很辛苦，但是 J. K. Rowling 還是持續寫她的書 while looking after her daughter. She enjoyed worldwide success finally.

1. ....

2. ....

TEST 44 詳解

1. *she got married there and later divorced.*【誤】（北一女中 李苡萱同學）

   * 句首須加連接詞 and。

   → where she $\left\{\begin{array}{l}\text{got married} \\ \text{married}\end{array}\right\}$ and $\left\{\begin{array}{l}\text{later} \\ \text{then}\end{array}\right\}$

   divorced.【正】

2. *Despite of the fact that life as a single mother was hard, J. K. Rowling still kept writing her books*【誤】（北一女中 李苡萱同學）

   * Despite of 須改為 In spite of 或 Despite。

   → $\left\{\begin{array}{l}\text{Despite her hard life} \\ \text{Although life was difficult}\end{array}\right\}$ as a single mother,

   J. K. Rowling $\left\{\begin{array}{l}\text{kept on} \\ \text{continued}\end{array}\right\}$ writing her book【正】

【註釋】 ***work as*** 擔任　　Portugal〔'portʃəgḷ〕*n.* 葡萄牙
   move〔muv〕*v.* 搬家
   Edinburgh〔'ɛdn̩ˏbɝo〕*n.* 愛丁堡【蘇格蘭的首府】
   Scotland〔'skɑtlənd〕*n.* 蘇格蘭
   look after 照顧　　enjoy〔ɪn'dʒɔɪ〕*v.* 享有
   worldwide〔'wɝld'waɪd〕*adj.* 全世界的
   divorce〔də'vɔrs〕*v.* 離婚
   despite〔dɪ'spaɪt〕*prep.* 儘管（= *in spite of*）
   single mother 單親媽媽

TEST 45

An American sailor fell in love with a Japanese girl.
Not knowing how to eat with chopsticks, he was afraid
to invite her to dinner. They just walked and talked and
never ate anything together. 1.為了克服這個困難，那個男子
去一家日本餐廳，要求服務生教他用筷子。 After practicing
for a while, he called the girl and asked her out to
dinner. The girl was very surprised, and she ran for
help immediately. 2.她乞求她的一位朋友教她如何用刀叉吃
東西。 When they met, the man was amazed that the
girl wanted to have Western food. From this story, we
know loving someone involves being willing to learn
new things. More than that, we need to overcome the
differences between us.

1. _____

2. _____

TEST 45 詳解

1. *In order to encounter the difficulty, the man went to a Japanese restaurant and asked the waiter to teach him use chopsticks.* 【誤】

（復興高中 蔡明倫同學）

* encounter（遭遇）須改為 overcome（克服），且 use 須改為 to use。

→ To overcome this difficulty, the man went to a Japanese restaurant and asked the waiter to teach him to use chopsticks. 【正】

2. *She begged one of her friends teached her eating food with knives and forks.* 【誤】（復興高中 蔡明倫同學）

* 須將 teached her eating 改為 to teach her to eat；knives and forks 須改為 a knife and fork。

→ She $\begin{cases} \text{begged} \\ \text{pleaded with} \end{cases}$ one of her friends to $\begin{cases} \text{teach} \\ \text{show} \end{cases}$ her how to eat with (a) knife and fork. 【正】

【註釋】 sailor〔ˋselɚ〕*n.* 水手　　***fall in love with*** 愛上
chopsticks〔ˋtʃɑpˏstɪks〕*n. pl.* 筷子
run for help 跑去找人幫忙
amazed〔əˋmezd〕*adj.* 驚訝的
involve〔ɪnˋvɑlv〕*v.* 需要　　willing〔ˋwɪlɪŋ〕*adj.* 願意的
overcome〔ˏovɚˋkʌm〕*v.* 克服　　beg〔bɛg〕*v.* 乞求
knife〔naɪf〕*n.* 刀子　　fork〔fɔrk〕*n.* 叉子
with (a) knife and fork 用刀叉

TEST 46

Sandboarding is an extreme sport that probably not many people know about. 1. 這項運動跟滑滑雪板及衝浪很類似，因為它需要絕佳的平衡感。 The sport is practiced in the desert, where sandboarders first bring their equipment up a slope. Before going down, it is important to make sure the boots are locked onto the board. Once the slide begins, it's hard to slow down because the sand is so loose. 2. 要注意的是隱藏在沙子裡的岩石。 If you are not careful, you might find yourself spinning in the air and landing head first in the sand.

1. ....

2. ....

TEST 46 詳解

1. *This kind of sport is similar to snowboarding and surffing, because it acquires great balance.*【誤】（中山女中 張庭瑄同學）

* surffing 拼錯，須改爲 surfing（衝浪），且 acquires（獲得）須改爲 requires（需要）。

→ $\left\{\begin{array}{l} \text{The} \\ \text{This} \end{array}\right\}$ sport is $\left\{\begin{array}{l} \text{similar to} \\ \text{like} \end{array}\right\}$ snowboarding and surfing $\left\{\begin{array}{l} \text{in that} \\ \text{because} \end{array}\right\}$ it $\left\{\begin{array}{l} \text{needs} \\ \text{requires} \end{array}\right\}$ $\left\{\begin{array}{l} \text{excellent} \\ \text{very good} \end{array}\right\}$ balance.【正】

2. *What you need to notice is the rocks which conceal in the sand.*【誤】
（中山女中 張庭瑄同學）

* conceal 須改爲被動語態 are concealed。

→ $\left.\begin{array}{l} \text{Something to watch out for} \\ \text{One thing to be careful of} \end{array}\right\}$ is rocks $\left\{\begin{array}{l} \text{hidden in} \\ \text{covered by} \end{array}\right\}$ the sand.【正】

【註釋】 sandboarding〔'sænd,bordɪŋ〕n. 滑沙
extreme〔ɪk'strim〕adj. 極限的　　desert〔'dɛzət〕n. 沙漠
sandboarder〔'sænd,bordə〕n. 滑沙的人
equipment〔ɪ'kwɪpmənt〕n. 裝備　　slope〔slop〕n. 斜坡
boots〔buts〕n. pl. 靴子　　lock〔lɑk〕v. 鎖
board〔bord〕n. 板子　　slide〔slaɪd〕n. 滑行
loose〔lus〕adj. 鬆的　　spin〔spɪn〕v. 旋轉
land〔lænd〕v. 著陸　　*head first* 頭朝下地
snowboarding〔'sno,bordɪŋ〕n. 滑滑雪板
surfing〔'sɜfɪŋ〕n. 衝浪　　*in that* 因爲
balance〔'bæləns〕n. 平衡　　*watch out for* 留意；注意

TEST 47

People around the world celebrate the arrival of a new baby in different ways. In America, for instance, friends or relatives of the new parents have a baby shower for them. Usually a baby shower is held in someone's home, but sometimes people celebrate the occasion at a restaurant, church, or park. In Chinese culture, 1. 傳統上當嬰兒滿月時，會發紅蛋或辦派對。 Proud parents often invite friends and relatives to their home to introduce them to the new baby. In Korea, many parents celebrate the first 100 days of a newborn with a large party, at which they pray and offer red bean cakes to the gods. 2. 有趣的是，紅豆糕對於韓國人，就像紅蛋對於中國人一樣重要。

1. ....

2. ....

TEST 47 詳解

1. *when a baby is…, people will give red eggs or throw a party.* 【誤】

（中山女中 郭彥汝同學）

＊「滿月」就是 is one month old，且 people will 應改為 it is
traditional to。

$$\rightarrow \text{it is} \left\{ \begin{array}{l} \text{traditional} \\ \text{a custom} \end{array} \right\} \text{to hand out red eggs or} \left\{ \begin{array}{l} \text{throw} \\ \text{hold} \\ \text{have} \end{array} \right\}$$

a party when the baby is one month old. 【正】

2. *Interestingly, red bean cakes to the Korean is as important as red eggs to the Chinese.* 【誤】 （中山女中 郭彥汝同學）

＊ to the Korean is as important as 須改為 are as important to the
Korean as；red eggs 之後須加 are。

→ Interestingly, red bean cakes are as important to the
Koreans as red eggs are to the Chinese. 【正】

或 It is interesting that the Koreans value red bean cakes
as much as the Chinese do red eggs. 【正】

【註釋】 *baby shower* 為新生嬰兒舉行的送禮會　　hold〔hold〕v. 舉行
occasion〔əˈkeʒən〕n. 場合；特別的大事
proud〔praʊd〕adj. 驕傲的　　Korea〔koˈriə〕n. 韓國
newborn〔ˈnjuˈbɔrn〕n. 新生兒　　*red bean* 紅豆
traditional〔trəˈdɪʃənḷ〕adj. 傳統的
hand out 分發　　*throw a party* 辦派對
interestingly〔ˈɪntrɪstɪŋlɪ〕adv. 有趣的是
Korean〔koˈriən〕adj. 韓國人的　　n. 韓國人
the Korean 韓國人（= the Koreans = Koreans）

TEST 48

説明：下面一段短文中，有數處係以中文呈現，請利用上下文線索（如單字、片語等）將其譯成正確、通順、達意且前後連貫的英文。

People have different ideas about what being popular means. For Andy, being popular meant belonging to a certain group in which everyone dressed similarly. Worried about being ignored by his friends, he tried to win popularity by copying other group members who looked cool even in the ugliest clothes. Every time the class held a group discussion or wrote a group report, he was quickly picked for a team. 1. 然而，他的那一組只是在鬼混，大部分的工作都沒做。 He was depressed and he came to realize that it was impossible for him to develop a close friendship with this group. He decided to keep his distance from them and learn to be himself. He believed that he could find people with the same interests as him. 2. 畢竟，忠於他自己比努力成為別人要來得好多了。

1. ....

2. ....

TEST 48　詳解

1. <u>*However, his group was just goofing around and didn't do most of the work.*</u>【誤】（北一女中　李律恩同學）

* do most of the work 須改為 do much of the work 或 do much work。

→ $\left.\begin{array}{l}\text{However,}\\\text{But}\end{array}\right\}$ his group just $\left\{\begin{array}{l}\text{fooled around}\\\text{wasted time}\end{array}\right\}$

   and $\left\{\begin{array}{l}\text{left most of the work undone.}\\\text{accomplished very little work.}\end{array}\right.$ 【正】

2. <u>*After all, sticking to himself was far better than making efforts to become others.*</u>【誤】（北一女中　李律恩同學）

* sticking to himself 須改成 being himself，而 to become others 須改成 to become like others。

→ $\left.\begin{array}{l}\text{After all,}\\\text{In the end,}\end{array}\right\}$ $\left\{\begin{array}{l}\text{being true to himself was much}\\\text{it was much better to be himself}\end{array}\right.$

   $\left.\begin{array}{l}\text{better than trying}\\\text{than to try}\end{array}\right\}$ to be someone else. 【正】

【註釋】　***belong to*** 屬於　　certain〔ˈsɝtn〕*adj.* 某個
similarly〔ˈsɪmələlɪ〕*adv.* 相似地　　ignore〔ɪgˈnor〕*v.* 忽視
popularity〔ˌpɑpjəˈlærətɪ〕*n.* 受歡迎　　copy〔ˈkɑpɪ〕*v.* 模仿
cool〔kul〕*adj.* 酷的　　ugly〔ˈʌglɪ〕*adj.* 醜的
pick〔pɪk〕*v.* 挑選　　team〔tim〕*n.* 團隊
depressed〔dɪˈprɛst〕*adj.* 沮喪的　　***come to V.*** （事情）演變到…
come to realize 發覺　　develop〔dɪˈvɛləp〕*v.* 培養
keep *one's* ***distance from*** 和～保持距離　　***fool around*** 鬼混
leave〔liv〕*v.* 使處於（某種狀態）　　***after all*** 畢竟

TEST 49

As a senior high school student, I think computers are really useful to me for two reasons. First, they help me a lot with my studies. For example, I can turn in my reports or homework through e-mail and get them back in the same way. I can also practice writing English compositions effectively 1.因為電腦不僅會指出我拼字上，還有文法上的錯 and even make them right. Writing on a computer is just like having a personal writing tutor.

Secondly, I can communicate with my friends through e-mail easily. I can type all my messages on the computer and then send them out. Usually, I can receive the replies quickly. Moreover, unlike talking on the phone, using a computer gives me more time to pick the right words. 2.此外，使用電子郵件比講電話更便宜。

1. ....

2. ....

TEST 49 詳解

1. *because computers can not only point out my fault on spelling but also on grammar*【誤】(建國中學 蔡定瑋同學)

   * can not only point out 須改成 can point out not only，且 on 均須改成 in。

   → because the computer will point out my mistakes

   $\left\{\begin{array}{l}\text{not only in spelling but also in grammar}\\\text{both in spelling and in grammar}\end{array}\right.$ 【正】

2. *Besides, using e-mail is cheaper than talking the phone.*【誤】

   (建國中學 蔡定瑋同學)

   * talking the phone 須改爲 talking on the phone（講電話）。

   $\left.\begin{array}{l}\text{Besides,}\\\text{→ In addition,}\\\text{Moreover,}\end{array}\right\}$ $\left\{\begin{array}{l}\text{using e-mail}\\\text{sending e-mail}\end{array}\right\}$ is $\left\{\begin{array}{l}\text{cheaper}\\\text{less expensive}\end{array}\right\}$

   than $\left\{\begin{array}{l}\text{talking on the telephone.}\\\text{making a phone call.}\end{array}\right.$ 【正】

【註釋】 ***turn in*** 繳交　　composition (ˌkɑmpəˈzɪʃən) *n.* 作文
   effectively (əˈfɛktɪvlɪ) *adv.* 有效地
   tutor (ˈtjutɚ) *n.* 家教
   communicate (kəˈmjunəˌket) *v.* 通信；連繫
   type (taɪp) *v.* 打字　　reply (rɪˈplaɪ) *n.* 回覆
   pick (pɪk) *v.* 挑選　　***point out*** 指出
   spelling (ˈspɛlɪŋ) *n.* 拼字
   grammar (ˈgræmɚ) *n.* 文法

TEST 50

Do you notice that children seem to learn a language easily and quickly? It's because children learn by doing what comes naturally. Children listen and understand what they hear. Then they mimic. In this way they learn how to use and speak the words of language. Children express themselves in simple words. <u>1.他們不在乎文法，或使用哪些字。</u> Instead, they just find ways to talk to others. Similarly, an English learner needs to listen to English as frequently as possible. For example, you can listen to an English radio program at your level every day. Also, try to find chances to talk to people in English. Don't be afraid of making mistakes. In short, <u>2.如果你想精通外語，你所必須做的，就是不斷地練習。</u>

1. ....

2. ....

TEST 50 詳解

1. *They don't care about grammer or using what words.* 【誤】

（和平高中 陳麒琛同學）

* grammer 拼錯，應改為 grammar（文法），且 using what words 須
改為 what words they use。

→ They {
don't care about
don't worry about
are not concerned about
} grammar or

{
which words they use.
vocabulary.
} 【正】

2. *if you want to master foreign language, all you have to do is*
keep practicing. 【誤】 （和平高中 陳麒琛同學）

* language 是可數名詞，故 foreign language 前須加 a。

→ if you want to {
master a foreign language,
learn another language well,
}

{
all you have to do is
you just have to
} practice {
constantly.
continuously.
} 【正】

【註釋】 come〔kʌm〕v. 出現；發生　　mimic〔'mɪmɪk〕v. 模仿
way〔we〕n. 方式　　express〔ɪk'sprɛs〕v. 表達
instead〔ɪn'stɛd〕adv. 取而代之；相反地
similarly〔'sɪmələlɪ〕adv. 同樣地　　*as…as possible* 儘可能…
level〔'lɛvl̩〕n. 程度　　*in short* 簡言之；總之
care about 關心；在乎　　grammar〔'græmə〕n. 文法
vocabulary〔və'kæbjəˌlɛrɪ〕n. 字彙　　master〔'mæstə〕v. 精通
all you have to do is V. 你所必須做的就是…
constantly〔'kɑnstəntlɪ〕adv. 不斷地

TEST 51

E-mail plays an important role in my daily life. I receive e-mails every day from my friends from all over the world. There are two major reasons for 1. 我用電子郵件，而不是電話或其他傳統的溝通方式。 There is no restriction on time or place. I can send messages whenever I have some thoughts to share with my friends. My friends can read my e-mails any time. If they happen to be online at the same time, I can get their reply immediately. How convenient! 2. 另一個理由就是電子郵件提供我一個結交朋友的新方法。 Since I am a shy person, I really have difficulty interacting with people face to face. With e-mail, I have plenty of time to think about what I want to say and choose the proper words.

1. ....

2. ....

TEST 51 詳解

1. *I use e-mail instead of phone calls or other conventional communication ways.*【誤】（內湖高中 顏佑安同學）

   * 因前有介系詞 for，故 I use 須改為 my using，而 phone calls 須改為 the phone，且 communication ways 須改為 ways of communication。

   $$\rightarrow \text{my using e-mail} \begin{Bmatrix} \text{instead of} \\ \text{rather than} \end{Bmatrix} \text{the phone or other}$$

   $$\begin{Bmatrix} \text{traditional} \\ \text{conventional} \end{Bmatrix} \begin{Bmatrix} \text{ways} \\ \text{means} \\ \text{methods} \end{Bmatrix} \text{of} \begin{Bmatrix} \text{communication.} \\ \text{communicating.} \end{Bmatrix}【正】$$

2. *Another reason is that e-mails provide me a new method to make friends.*【誤】（內湖高中 顏佑安同學）

   * e-mail（電子郵件）為不可數名詞，故 e-mails provide 須改為 e-mail provides，又 provide 的用法為：provide *sb.* with *sth.*，故 me 之後須加 with。

   → The other reason is (that) e-mail offers me a new way to make friends.【正】

   【註釋】 e-mail〔ˋiˏmel〕*n.* 電子郵件　　role〔rol〕*n.* 角色
   　　　　major〔ˋmedʒɚ〕*adj.* 主要的　　restriction〔rɪˋstrɪkʃən〕*n.* 限制
   　　　　message〔ˋmɛsɪdʒ〕*n.* 訊息　　share〔ʃɛr〕*v.* 分享
   　　　　happen to 碰巧　　online〔ˋɑnˏlaɪn〕*adv.* 在線上
   　　　　reply〔rɪˋplaɪ〕*n.* 回覆　　shy〔ʃaɪ〕*adj.* 害羞的
   　　　　have difficulty + (*in*) + *V-ing* 很難…
   　　　　interact〔ˏɪntɚˋækt〕*v.* 互動　　***face to face*** 面對面
   　　　　plenty of 很多　　proper〔ˋprɑpɚ〕*adj.* 適當的
   　　　　traditional〔trəˋdɪʃənḷ〕*adj.* 傳統的　　means〔minz〕*n.* 方法

TEST 52

People who want to stay at the ice hotel need to be aware of two things. First, the hotel is open only in winter. <u>1. 因為它是由雪和冰所製成的，所以，很快地，當春天來臨，然後最後是夏天，</u> the rooms, the suites, the bar, the reception, in fact the entire creation, will disappear. Second, being properly dressed is the key to experiencing the unique sensation of staying in an ice hotel. <u>2. 穿足夠保暖的衣服是很重要的，而且應該要避免棉質的衣服。</u> Because cotton binds moisture, it has the effect of chilling you instead of warming you. Thus, wearing cotton clothing in the ice hotel will get you in trouble.

1. ....

2. ....

TEST 52 詳解

1. *Because it is made up of snow and ices, so, soon, when spring comes, then summer is the last,*【誤】（建國中學 鄭維同學）

   * ices 須改為 ice，且因為前有連接詞 Because，故須將 so, 去掉，而 summer is the last 須改為 then finally the summer。

   → $\left.\begin{array}{l} \text{Since} \\ \text{Because} \end{array}\right\}$ it is made of snow and ice, very soon,

   when spring comes, then finally the summer,【正】

2. *Wearing sufficient-warm clothes is so crucial, and we should avoid wearing cotton-made clothes.*【誤】（建國中學 鄭維同學）

   * sufficient-warm 須改為 sufficiently warm，又 crucial 即表「非常重要的」，前面不須加 so，且 cotton-made 須改為 cotton（棉製的）。

   → $\left.\begin{array}{l} \text{Wearing enough warm clothes} \\ \text{Dressing warmly} \end{array}\right\}$ is important,

   and cotton $\left\{\begin{array}{l} \text{clothing} \\ \text{garments} \end{array}\right\}$ should be avoided.【正】

【註釋】 stay〔ste〕v. 暫住　**be aware of** 知道；察覺到
suite〔swit〕n. 套房　reception〔rɪ'sɛpʃən〕n.（旅館的）櫃台
creation〔krɪ'eʃən〕n. 產物；作品
be properly dressed 穿著適當　key〔ki〕n. 關鍵
experience〔ɪk'spɪrɪəns〕v. 體驗
unique〔ju'nik〕adj. 獨特的　sensation〔sɛn'seʃən〕n. 感覺
cotton〔'kɑtn̩〕n. 棉　adj. 棉製的　bind〔baɪnd〕v. 使凝固
moisture〔'mɔɪstʃɚ〕n. 濕氣；水蒸氣
effect〔ɪ'fɛkt〕n. 效果　chill〔tʃɪl〕v. 使（人）感覺寒冷
get sb. **in trouble** 使某人惹上麻煩

TEST 53

說明：下面一段短文中，有數處係以中文呈現，請利用上下文線索（如單字、片語等）將其譯成正確、通順、達意且前後連貫的英文。

My family was happy until one January day. That morning I heard my mom screaming my name. When I saw tears in her eyes and her terrified look, I knew something was really wrong. 1. 我跑下樓，發現我父親在地下室，坐在椅子上， his limp body supported by my brother. The medics soon rushed him to the hospital. I felt so scared and so sorry. I prayed to God and finally my prayer was answered. Since then, I have realized that nothing is ever certain. Now I firmly believe that 2. 只有當某樣東西被奪走時，你才會了解自己擁有了什麼。

1. ....

2. ....

TEST 53 詳解

1. *I ran down the floor and found my father sitting on the chair in the basement,*【誤】（景美女中 張晴茹同學）

   * 須將 floor 改成 stairs（樓梯），且 on the chair 須改為 on a chair。

   → I $\left\{\begin{array}{l}\text{ran downstairs} \\ \text{raced down the stairs}\end{array}\right\}$ and found my father

   in the basement $\left\{\begin{array}{l}\text{sitting on a chair,} \\ \text{seated on a chair,}\end{array}\right.$ 【正】

2. *only when something are taken, you will realize what you have.*【誤】（景美女中 張晴茹同學）

   * something 為單數代名詞，故 are taken 須改為 is taken，且 only when 置於句首，主詞與動詞須倒裝，故 you will 須改為 do you。

   → $\left.\begin{array}{l}\text{only when} \\ \text{not until}\end{array}\right\}$ something is taken away

   do you $\left\{\begin{array}{l}\text{realize} \\ \text{understand}\end{array}\right\}$ what you have. 【正】

【註釋】 scream〔skrim〕v. 尖叫　　tear〔tɪr〕n. 眼淚
terrible〔'tɛrəbl̩〕adj. 可怕的　　look〔lʊk〕n. 樣子
limp〔lɪmp〕adj. 軟弱的；無力氣的
support〔sə'port〕v. 支持；支撐　　medic〔'mɛdɪk〕n. 醫生
rush sb. to the hospital 趕緊把某人送進醫院
scared〔skɛrd〕adj. 害怕的　　pray〔pre〕v. 祈禱
prayer〔prɛr〕n. 禱告；祈禱
answer〔'ænsɚ〕v. 答應；允許　　ever〔'ɛvɚ〕adv. 總是；始終
downstairs〔'daʊn'stɛrz〕adv. 到樓下
race〔res〕v. 疾行；快跑　　basement〔'besmənt〕n. 地下室

TEST 54

When we interact with people on social occasions, there are many unspoken signals that help us send out nonverbal messages to express our feelings. Smiling, for one, implies our contentment, and crying, for another, shows our sadness. These kinds of emotional responses are often considered innate because we don't have to learn them; they just come naturally. <u>1. 然而，仍然有很多其他形式的肢體語言，每個文化都不同。</u> For example, the hand signal for "O.K." in America symbolizes money in Japan. Misunderstanding may arise if people with different cultural backgrounds ignore these differences. <u>2. 事實上，在任何文化，非語言的訊息的重要性，再怎麼強調也不為過。</u>

1. ....

2. ....

TEST 54 詳解

1. _However, there are still many other forms of body languages which differ from one culture to another._【誤】(西松高中 張靜婷同學)

   * languages 須改為 language。

   → However, there are still many other forms of body language that $\begin{Bmatrix} \text{vary} \\ \text{differ} \end{Bmatrix}$ from culture to culture. 【正】

2. _In fact, in every culture, the importance of non-verbal message cannot be overenphasized._【誤】(西松高中 張靜婷同學)

   * message 為可數名詞，故須改為 messages，而 overenphasized 拼錯，應改為 overemphasized。

   → In fact, the importance of nonverbal messages cannot be overemphasized in any culture. 【正】

【註釋】 interact〔͵ɪntə͞ˋækt〕v. 互動　　social〔ˋsoʃəl〕adj. 社交的
occasion〔əˋkeʒən〕n. 場合
unspoken〔ʌnˋspokən〕adj. 未說出口的　　**send out** 發出
nonverbal〔ˋnɑnˋvɝbḷ〕adj. 非言辭的　　**for one** 舉一個例子
imply〔ɪmˋplaɪ〕v. 暗示　　contentment〔kənˋtɛntmənt〕n. 滿足
emotional〔ɪˋmoʃənḷ〕adj. 情緒的
response〔rɪˋspɑns〕n. 反應　　innate〔ɪˋnet〕adj. 天生的
come〔kʌm〕v. 出現　　symbolize〔ˋsɪmbḷ͵aɪz〕v. 象徵
arise〔əˋraɪz〕v. 產生　　background〔ˋbæk͵graʊnd〕n. 背景
ignore〔ɪgˋnor〕v. 忽視　　vary〔ˋvɛrɪ〕v. 不同
vary from culture to culture 每個文化都不同
the importance of~cannot be overemphasized ～的重要性
　　再怎麼強調也不為過

TEST 55

1. 當一隻企鵝生氣了，而另一隻沒生氣時，沒生氣的那一隻會不看另一隻 and will walk away with its head and body held very low. When Little Penguins want to attract a boyfriend or girlfriend, they will show they like the boy or girl by imitating what they do, or by cleaning the boy or girl penguin's feathers. The Little Penguins are fascinating to watch. 2. 難怪牠們在澳洲已經成為最受喜愛的動物之一！

1. ....

2. ....

TEST 55 詳解

1. <u>*When one penguin is angry and the other is not, the one who is not angry won't look at the other*</u> 【誤】（北一女中 黃孺雅同學）

* who 須改為 that 或 which。

→ When one penguin is $\begin{Bmatrix} \text{angry} \\ \text{upset} \end{Bmatrix}$ and the other one

is not, the one that is not angry will not look at

the other 【正】

2. <u>*No wonder that they have already been one of the most lovely animals in Australia!*</u>【誤】（北一女中 黃孺雅同學）

* have already been 須改為 have already become，且 most lovely
須改為 most-loved (最受喜愛的)。

→ $\begin{rcases} \text{No wonder} \\ \text{It is no surprise that} \end{rcases}$ they have become one of the

$\begin{Bmatrix} \text{most-loved} \\ \text{favorite} \end{Bmatrix}$ animals in Australia! 【正】

【註釋】　hold〔hold〕*v.* 使處於（某種狀態）

penguin〔'pɛngwɪn〕*n.* 企鵝

imitate〔'ɪmə,tet〕*v.* 模仿　　feather〔'fɛðɚ〕*n.* 羽毛

fascinating〔'fæsn̩,etɪŋ〕*adj.* 迷人的；很有趣的

no wonder 難怪

most-loved〔'most,lʌvd〕*adj.* 最受喜愛的

TEST 56

People of every race and culture enjoy eating bread. 1. 麵包的起源可追溯至石器時代。 People collected wheat, which could be stored for long periods of time. It was likely that they only chewed the wheat at first. Soon after, they realized that they could make dough by mixing wheat with water. Then, they cooked this dough over fires to make hard bread. The hard bread was not easy to eat, but our ancestors soon discovered the solution. When the uncooked dough was left out for many hours, it attracted natural yeast. 2. 酵母菌使得麵糰膨脹，並使它變得較軟，而且比較容易嚼。 After that, bread quickly became a big part of people's diet.

1. ....

2. ....

TEST 56 詳解

1. *Bread can be traced back to the stone era.* 【誤】（建國中學 張淳富同學）

   * 句首應加上 The origin of，且 Bread 須改為 bread；the stone era
   須改為 the Stone Age（石器時代）。

   → Bread's beginnings $\left\{ \begin{array}{l} \text{go back to} \\ \text{can be traced back to} \end{array} \right\}$

   the Stone Age. 【正】

   或 The origin of bread $\left\{ \begin{array}{l} \text{goes back to} \\ \text{can be traced back to} \end{array} \right\}$

   the Stone Age. 【正】

2. *Yeast make dough bluffy, softer and easier to chew.* 【誤】

   （建國中學 張淳富同學）

   * make 須改為 made，且 bluffy 須改為 fluffy（蓬鬆的）。

   → The yeast $\left\{ \begin{array}{l} \text{caused the dough to rise} \\ \text{made the dough rise} \end{array} \right\}$

   and made it softer and easier to chew. 【正】

【註釋】　race〔res〕n. 種族　　　wheat〔hwit〕n. 小麥
　　　　　store〔stor〕v. 儲存　　　chew〔tʃu〕v. 嚼
　　　　　dough〔do〕n. 麵糰　　　mix〔mɪks〕v. 混合
　　　　　ancestor〔'ænsɛstɚ〕n. 祖先　solution〔sə'luʃən〕n. 解決之道
　　　　　be left out 被留在外面　　yeast〔jist〕n. 酵母（菌）
　　　　　diet〔'daɪət〕n. 飲食　　　beginnings〔bɪ'gɪnɪŋz〕n. pl. 起源
　　　　　go back to 可追溯到（= *can be traced back to*）
　　　　　origin〔'ɔrədʒɪn〕n. 起源　　fluffy〔'flʌfɪ〕adj. 蓬鬆的
　　　　　cause〔kɔz〕v. 使　　　　rise〔raɪz〕v.（麵包）膨脹；發起來

TEST 57

In November the cold, wet weather brought sickness to the neighborhood where the two women lived, and one of them, Joanna, became very ill with pneumonia. She lay on her bed, looking through the windows at the side of the next brick building. After the doctor had gone, her friend, Sue, cried and cried. Finally she walked into Joanna's room and 1. 發現她躺在床上，眼睛張得大大的。 She had given up hope of living. But because of their neighbor, Mr. Behrman, 2. 喬安娜發現了她生命中的希望，並從肺炎中復元。

1. ....

2. ....

TEST 57 詳解

1. <u>*found her lying on the bed with her eyes opened wide.*</u> 【誤】

(建國中學 黃上瑋同學)

* opened wide 須改為 wide open 或 wide opened。

→ found／discovered ⎬ her lying on the bed, with her eyes

wide open. 【正】

2. <u>*Joanna discovered the hope in her life and recovered from the pneumonia.*</u> 【誤】 (建國中學 黃上瑋同學)

* the hope 須改為 hope。

→ Joanna found hope in her life and

⎧ recovered from pneumonia.
⎨ get over the pneumonia. 【正】

【註釋】 neighborhood〔'nebəˌhʊd〕*n.* 鄰近地區

pneumonia〔nju'monɪə〕*n.* 肺炎

brick〔brɪk〕*adj.* 磚造的

give up 放棄 recover〔rɪ'kʌvɚ〕*v.* 恢復

get over 自…康復

TEST 58

Imagine that all of us have a bank called Time. Every day it credits you with 86,400 seconds. Every night, it writes off, as lost, whatever part of the balance you fail to use during that day. There is no drawing against "tomorrow". 1. 你必須好好投資你的時間，以便善加利用每天的帳戶。 To realize the value of a year, ask a student who failed a grade. To understand the value of a millisecond, 2. 問那個在奧運會中贏得銀牌的人。 We must live in the present on today's deposits.

1. ....

2. ....

TEST 58 詳解

1. *You have to invest your time well to make the best of daily account.*【誤】（師大附中 鄭文淇同學）

* make the best of 須改爲 make the most of (善加利用)。

→ You $\left\{ \begin{array}{l} \text{must} \\ \text{have to} \end{array} \right\}$ invest your time well $\left\{ \begin{array}{l} \text{so as to} \\ \text{in order to} \end{array} \right\}$

$\left\{ \begin{array}{l} \text{make the most of} \\ \text{get everything you can out of} \end{array} \right\}$ your daily account. 【正】

2. *ask the one who wins the silver medal in the Olimpic Games.*【誤】

（師大附中 鄭文淇同學）

* Olimpic 拼錯，須改爲 Olympic。

→ ask the person who won a silver medal in the

$\left\{ \begin{array}{l} \text{Olympics.} \\ \text{Olympic Games.} \end{array} \right.$ 【正】

【註釋】 imagine〔ɪ'mædʒɪn〕v. 想像

credit〔'krɛdɪt〕v. 信用貸款給…

second〔'sɛkənd〕n. 秒　*write off* 把…註銷

lost〔lɔst〕adj. 失去的　balance〔'bæləns〕n. 餘額

fail to V. 無法~　*fail a grade* 留級

millisecond〔'mɪlə,sɛkənd〕n. 毫秒；千分之一秒

present〔'prɛznt〕n. 目前

deposit〔dɪ'pɑzɪt〕n. 存款　invest〔ɪn'vɛst〕v. 投資

make the most of 善用　daily〔'delɪ〕adj. 每天的

account〔ə'kaʊnt〕n. 帳戶　*silver medal* 銀牌

Olympics〔o'lɪmpɪks〕n. 奧運會 (= the Olympic Games)

TEST 59

Taiwan is a paradise for people who like to eat out. Whenever you feel hungry, it is easy and convenient to find something to eat. It doesn't matter what you want to eat or how much money you want to spend, there is always something that meets your needs. Among the various choices, 1. 小吃攤特別方便，因此深受大家歡迎。 When you are in a hurry and don't want to spend too much time eating, you can just stop at any food stand on the sidewalk and in a minute you can enjoy the delicious dishes that you order. What's more, food stands are also the best choices for budget meals. 2. 用很少的錢，你就能在所提供的各種食物中，選擇你喜歡的 and eat to your heart's content.

1. ....

2. ....

TEST 59 詳解

1. *vendors are especially convenient, so they're popular.* 【誤】

（中山女中 張若芃同學）

* vendors 須改為 food vendors；而 popular 之前須加副詞 very。

→ food $\begin{Bmatrix} \text{stands} \\ \text{vendors} \end{Bmatrix}$ are especially convenient

$\begin{cases} \text{and therefore popular with people.} \\ \text{, so they are very popular.} \end{cases}$ 【正】

2. *With little money, you can choose the one you like among the variety of food provided* 【誤】 （中山女中 張若芃同學）

* the one 須改為 what；而 among 須改為 from。

→ With little money, you can $\begin{Bmatrix} \text{choose} \\ \text{select} \end{Bmatrix}$ what you like

from the $\begin{Bmatrix} \text{various} \\ \text{many} \end{Bmatrix}$ kinds of food offered 【正】

【註釋】 paradise〔'pærə,daɪz〕 n. 天堂　　*eat out* 出去吃

meet〔mit〕 v. 滿足　　various〔'vɛrɪəs〕 adj. 各種的

in a hurry 匆忙　　*food stand* 小吃攤

sidewalk〔'saɪd,wɔk〕 n. 人行道

in a minute 立刻　　dish〔dɪʃ〕 n. 菜餚

order〔'ɔrdə〕 v. 點（菜）　　*what's more* 此外

budget〔'bʌdʒɪt〕 adj. 便宜的；特價的

to one's heart's content 盡情地

vendor〔'vɛndə〕 n. 小販

TEST 60

In Japan, people love baseball. When you go to a game there, you may be surprised by the behavior of the fans. 1. 他們真的很大聲，而且他們所製造的噪音會持續不停。 They cheer, chant, bang on drums and blow trumpets throughout the game, even if their team is losing badly. Going to a baseball game is a lot of fun in Japan.

It is also exciting in Taiwan, where fans can be just as loud. Here, fans cheer their team on using air horns. These can really hurt your ears if you are sitting close to them. 2. 台灣的球迷也很喜歡大叫來刺激與鼓勵球員。

1. ....

2. ....

TEST 60 詳解

1. *They are really aloud, and the noise they made will be constant.*【誤】（建國中學 吳芳育同學）

   * aloud（出聲地）須改爲 loud（大聲的），且依句意爲現在式，故 made 須改爲 make。

   → They are really loud, and the noise they make
   $\left\{\begin{array}{l}\text{continues nonstop.} \\ \text{goes on and on.}\end{array}\right.$【正】

2. *The fans in Taiwan also likes to shout to stimulate and cheer the players.*【誤】（建國中學 吳芳育同學）

   * fans 爲複數名詞，故 likes 須改爲 like。

   → $\left\{\begin{array}{l}\text{Taiwanese fans} \\ \text{Fans in Taiwan}\end{array}\right\}$ $\left\{\begin{array}{l}\text{also like to yell a lot to excite} \\ \text{like to excite and encourage}\end{array}\right.$

   $\left.\begin{array}{l}\text{and encourage the players.} \\ \text{the players by yelling, too.}\end{array}\right\}$【正】

【註釋】 behavior〔bɪˈhevjə〕*n.* 行爲　　fan〔fæn〕*n.* 球迷
　　　　cheer〔tʃɪr〕*v.* 歡呼；激勵
　　　　chant〔tʃænt〕*v.* 詠唱；反覆地說
　　　　bang〔bæŋ〕*v.* 重擊；猛擊
　　　　drum〔drʌm〕*n.* 鼓　　trumpet〔ˈtrʌmpɪt〕*n.* 喇叭
　　　　throughout〔θruˈaʊt〕*prep.* 遍及
　　　　even if 即使　　*lose badly* 輸得很慘
　　　　fun〔fʌn〕*n.* 樂趣　　*cheer～on* 鼓舞～；聲援～
　　　　air horn 氣笛喇叭　　nonstop〔ˈnɑnˈstɑp〕*adv.* 不停地

TEST 61

說明：下面一段短文中，有數處係以中文呈現，請利用上下文線索（如單字、片語等）將其譯成正確、通順、達意且前後連貫的英文。

A critical thinker considers an issue from different perspectives. Getting different perspectives on an issue can open up your mind to new ways of thinking. One way to do this is to ask different people what they think. Hearing others' opinions may cause your own to change or may make them become even more solid.

1. 當該做決定的時候，要仔細考慮所有不同選擇的利與弊。

Once you have made a decision, you may have to win others over to your way of thinking. Take heart; you have reached your decision using critical thinking.

2. 你可以告知別人你做決定的過程，他們也可能會被說服。

1. ....

2. ....

TEST 61 詳解

1. *When making decisions, you have to consider the pros and cons of all kinds of decisions carefully.* 【誤】（北一女中 曹如謹同學）

* When making 須改為 When it's time to make，且 all kinds of decisions 須改為 all kinds of choices。

→ $\left.\begin{array}{l}\text{When it's time} \\ \text{When the time comes}\end{array}\right\}$ to make a decision,

$\left\{\begin{array}{l}\text{think over} \\ \text{think about}\end{array}\right\}$ the $\left\{\begin{array}{l}\text{pros and cons} \\ \text{advantages and disadvantages}\end{array}\right\}$

of all the different $\left\{\begin{array}{l}\text{choices.} \\ \text{options.}\end{array}\right.$ 【正】

2. *You can tell others your process of making decisions, and they may be pursuaded.* 【誤】（北一女中 曹如謹同學）

* your process of making decisions 須改為 your decision-making process，且 pursuaded 拼錯，應改為 persuaded。

→ You can $\left\{\begin{array}{l}\text{inform others of your decision-making process} \\ \text{tell other people how you made the decision}\end{array}\right\}$

and they may be $\left\{\begin{array}{l}\text{convinced.} \\ \text{persuaded.}\end{array}\right.$ 【正】

【註釋】 critical〔ˋkrɪtɪk!〕*adj.* 批判性的　　consider（kənˋsɪdɚ）*v.* 考慮
issue〔ˋɪʃjʊ〕*n.* 問題　　perspective（pɚˋspɛktɪv）*n.* 看法；觀點
cause〔kɔz〕*v.* 使　　solid〔ˋsɑlɪd〕*adj.* 正確的；有根據的
win sb. over to ~ 說服某人贊成~　　***take heart*** 振作精神
the pros and cons 利與弊；優缺點　　option〔ˋɑpʃən〕*n.* 選擇
inform（ɪnˋfɔrm）*v.* 通知；告知　　process（ˋprɑsɛs）*n.* 過程
convince（kənˋvɪns）*v.* 說服（= *persuade*）

TEST 62

説明：下面一段短文中，有數處係以中文呈現，請利用上下文線索（如單字、片語等）將其譯成正確、通順、達意且前後連貫的英文。

Acupuncture is a treatment for pain and illness. 1. 在典型的治療中，醫生會將針插入病人的身體裡。 The needles will not be inserted in the place where the patient feels pain, but at special points that match the body's flow of energy. The patient will feel a slight pinch instead of great pain when each needle goes in. According to the ancient Chinese, energy flowed through the human body along certain paths. Either too much or too little energy flowing to one part of the body would lead to pain or illness. They believed 2. 針灸的針可以改變能量的流動，使它流得很平順。 As a result, the patient would feel better and become healthy again.

1. ....

2. ....

TEST 62 詳解

1. <u>*In the classical treatment, the doctor will inserted the needle*</u>
<u>*in the patient's body.*</u>【誤】（中正高中 黃工哲同學）

* will 是助動詞，其後的動詞須用原形，故 inserted 須改為 insert。

→ In a typical treatment, the doctor $\begin{Bmatrix} \text{inserts needles into} \\ \text{places needles in} \end{Bmatrix}$

the patient's body.【正】

2. <u>*the needle will change the flow of the energy and make it*</u>
<u>*smoothly.*</u>【誤】（中正高中 黃工哲同學）

* the needle 須改為 acupuncture needles，且 will 須改為 could，又
smoothly 須改為形容詞 smooth，做受詞補語。

→ acupuncture needles could change the flow of energy
and make it flow smoothly.【正】

【註釋】 acupuncture (ˈækjʊˌpʌŋktʃɚ) *n.* 針灸
treatment (ˈtritmənt) *n.* 治療法
insert (ɪnˈsɝt) *v.* 插入   point (pɔɪnt) *n.* 某一點
match (mætʃ) *v.* 與～一致；配合   flow (flo) *n.* 流動
energy (ˈɛnɚdʒɪ) *n.* 能量；活力
slight (slaɪt) *adj.* 稍微的
pinch (pɪntʃ) *n.* 擠痛；不舒服
certain (ˈsɝtn̩) *adj.* 某些   path (pæθ) *n.* 路徑
lead to 導致   ***as a result*** 因此
typical (ˈtɪpɪkl̩) *adj.* 典型的
smoothly (ˈsmuðlɪ) *adv.* 平順地

TEST 63

You just never know what girls are thinking. One minute they are happy 1. 而且下一分鐘她們看起來就好像在生氣。 Yesterday, when I called my girlfriend, she hung up on me without saying goodbye. My friend Jack said that I might have made her angry because I said something stupid, 2. 並且我最好回電話給她，並向她道歉。 But I don't know what to say if I call her. I don't even know what I did wrong.

1. ....

2. ....

TEST 63 詳解

1. *, and the next minute, they looks angry.*【誤】（內湖高中 郭子模同學）

   * looks 須改為 look。

   → and the next minute they look $\begin{cases} \text{as if} \\ \text{as though} \end{cases}$

   they are $\begin{cases} \text{offended.} \\ \text{angry.} \end{cases}$ 【正】

2. *and I'd better call her to apologize.*【誤】（內湖高中 郭子模同學）

   * 依句意，and 須改為 and that，在 My friend Jack said that…and that…句中的第二個 that 不可省；而「回她電話」是 call her back，故須在 her 後面加 back。

   → and that I had better call her back

   and $\begin{cases} \text{apologize to her.} \\ \text{tell her that I was sorry.} \end{cases}$ 【正】

【註釋】 ***hang up on*** *sb.* 掛某人電話
   stupid〔'stjupɪd〕*adj.* 愚蠢的　　***as if*** 就好像
   offend〔ə'fɛnd〕*v.* 冒犯；觸怒
   call *sb.* ***back*** 回某人電話
   apologize〔ə'palə,dʒaɪz〕*v.* 道歉

TEST 64

In order to help the pupa in a cocoon to get out, a man took a pair of scissors and enlarged the opening of the cocoon. The butterfly came out with ease, but it had a swollen body and shriveled wings. In fact, it was never able to fly <u>1.因為蝴蝶需要在通過蠶蛹上的小洞所做的掙扎。</u> From this lesson, we can learn that sometimes struggles are just what we need in our life. <u>2.如果上帝讓我們過著沒有任何阻礙的生活，</u> it would cripple us and we would never be able to face difficulties and grow up.

1. ....

2. ....

TEST 64 詳解

1. *because the butterfly need struggles when passes the little hole of cocoon.* 【誤】

   * need struggles when passes 須改為 need the struggle to pass through。

   → because the butterfly $\begin{cases} \text{required the struggle} \\ \text{needed to fight} \end{cases}$ to get

   through the $\begin{cases} \text{narrow} \\ \text{small} \end{cases}$ opening of the cocoon. 【正】

2. *If god lets us to live a life without any obstacles,* 【誤】

   * god (神) 須改為 God (上帝),且依句意為「與現在事實相反的假設」,故動詞須用過去式,lets 須改為 let,to live 須改為 live。

   → If God $\begin{cases} \text{allowed us to lead} \\ \text{let us live} \end{cases}$ our lives

   $\begin{cases} \text{without any} \\ \text{with no} \end{cases}$ obstacles, 【正】

   【註釋】 pupa (ˈpjupə) n. 蛹   cocoon (kəˈkun) n. 繭
   scissors (ˈsɪzəz) n. pl. 剪刀   *a pair of scissors* 一把剪刀
   enlarge (ɪnˈlɑrdʒ) v. 加大   opening (ˈopənɪŋ) n. 口;孔
   butterfly (ˈbʌtəˌflaɪ) n. 蝴蝶   *with ease* 輕易地
   swollen (ˈswolən) adj. 膨脹的;腫大的
   shriveled (ˈʃrɪvḷd) adj. 萎縮的;捲縮的   wing (wɪŋ) n. 翅膀
   lesson (ˈlɛsṇ) n. 教訓   struggle (ˈstrʌgḷ) n. 掙扎
   cripple (ˈkrɪpḷ) v. 使殘弱;削弱   require (rɪˈkwaɪr) v. 需要
   lead a~life 過著~生活 (= *live a~life*)
   obstacle (ˈɑbstəkḷ) n. 阻礙

TEST 65

1. 儘管時代已經改變了，現在美國的新娘仍然會按照這句俗語來打扮： "Something old, something new, something borrowed, something blue." The family jewels she often wears are a symbol of her close relationship with her family. It's also traditional that the bride wear at least one new item, which stands for a wish for good luck in her new life. The bride's tossing of the bouquet is also important. 2. 凡是在喜筵結束時接到它的人，可能就會是下一個新娘。 Last but not least, the bride should be the best-dressed person at the wedding. Therefore, it's considered impolite to dress more beautifully than the bride.

1. ....

2. ....

TEST 65 詳解

1. <u>*Although the generation has changed, now the America's*</u>
<u>*bride still dressed by the saying:*</u>【誤】（華僑高中 張維哲同學）

* the generation has 須改爲 the times have；America's 須改爲
  American；依句意爲現在式，故 dressed 須改爲 dresses；
  by 須改爲 according to。

$$\rightarrow \left\{ \begin{array}{l} \text{Despite the fact that} \\ \text{Although} \end{array} \right\} \text{times have changed,}$$

American brides today still dress themselves
according to the saying: 【正】

2. <u>*Everyone who caught you after the banquet, she may become*</u>
<u>*the next bride.*</u>【誤】（華僑高中 張維哲同學）

* Everyone who…banquet, she 須改爲 Whoever catches it at the end
  of the wedding banquet。

$$\rightarrow \left\{ \begin{array}{l} \text{Whoever catches it} \\ \text{The one who catches the bouquet} \end{array} \right\} \text{at the end of the}$$

wedding reception $\left\{ \begin{array}{l} \text{might} \\ \text{may} \end{array} \right\}$ be the next bride. 【正】

【註釋】 jewel（'dʒuəl）*n.* 珠寶   symbol（'sɪmbl̩）*n.* 象徵
close（klos）*adj.* 親密的   traditional（trə'dɪʃənl̩）*adj.* 傳統的
item（'aɪtəm）*n.* 物品   *stand for* 代表
tossing（'tɔsɪŋ）*n.* 投擲   bouquet（bu'ke）*n.* 花束
last but not least 最後一項要點是   wedding（'wɛdɪŋ）*n.* 婚禮
despite（dɪ'spaɪt）*prep.* 儘管   saying（'seɪŋ）*n.* 俗語
wedding reception 喜筵（= *wedding banquet*）

TEST 66

International signs can be understood easily no matter what language people speak. No language is necessary to know what they mean. 1.國際的標誌對於在各國旅行的人而言，的確很有幫助。 Most travelers can immediately recognize signs for a luggage cart or a phone even if they don't know how to say or spell the words. However, there are many situations in which an important message is delivered through language, such as signs that say "Entrance" or "Danger". 2.因此，爲了了解這些標誌，我們必須懂這些單字以及符號。

1. ......

2. ......

TEST 66 詳解

1. <u>*International signs are really helpful for every people who go abroad around the world.*</u>【誤】（三民高中 杜長恩同學）

   * 須將 every 去掉，且 who go abroad...world 須改為 who travel from country to country。

   → International signs really are $\begin{cases} \text{a great help} \\ \text{of great assistance} \end{cases}$

   to $\begin{cases} \text{people traveling from country to country.} \\ \text{international travelers.} \end{cases}$ 【正】

2. <u>*Therefore, in order to realize these signs, we have to understand these vocabularies and the symbols.*</u>【誤】（三民高中 杜長恩同學）

   * realize 須改為 understand，且 vocabulary 為不可數名詞，故 vocabularies 須改為 words。

   → $\begin{cases} \text{To} \\ \text{In order to} \end{cases}$ $\begin{cases} \text{understand these signs,} \\ \text{know what the signs mean,} \end{cases}$ therefore,

   we $\begin{cases} \text{have to} \\ \text{must} \end{cases}$ $\begin{cases} \text{know} \\ \text{understand} \end{cases}$ the words as well as

   the symbols. 【正】

   【註釋】 sign〔saɪn〕*n.* 標誌　recognize〔'rɛkəɡ,naɪz〕*v.* 認得
   luggage〔'lʌɡɪdʒ〕*n.* 行李　cart〔kɑrt〕*n.* 手推車
   message〔'mɛsɪdʒ〕*n.* 訊息
   deliver〔dɪ'lɪvɚ〕*v.* 遞送；傳達　*such as* 像是
   say〔se〕*v.* 寫著　entrance〔'ɛntrəns〕*n.* 入口
   as well as 以及　symbol〔'sɪmbl̩〕*n.* 象徵；符號

TEST 67

說明：下面一段短文中，有數處係以中文呈現，請利用上下
文線索（如單字、片語等）將其譯成正確、通順、達
意且前後連貫的英文。

Walking on the street, I saw my ex-girlfriend talking joyfully with an ugly but rich guy. My heart was broken. The way she looked at him showed her great love for him. How I wish I were him! 1. 如果我多注意她，她上星期就不會和我分手了。 If I had agreed to marry her before she was thirty, she wouldn't have handed me the Dear John letter. 2. 如果我還有一次機會，我不會犯同樣的錯誤，放開她的手。

1. ....

2. ....

TEST 67 詳解

1. *If I had paid more attention to her, she wouldn't have broke up
   with me last week.*【誤】 (延平高中 張育維同學)

   * 須將 broke 改爲過去分詞 broken。

   → If I had $\left\{\begin{array}{l}\text{given her more attention,} \\ \text{paid more attention to her,}\end{array}\right\}$ she wouldn't

   have $\left\{\begin{array}{l}\text{split up} \\ \text{broken up}\end{array}\right\}$ with me last week. 【正】

2. *If I had a chance once again, I won't make the same
   mistake…*【誤】 (延平高中 張育維同學)

   * a chance once again 須改爲 another chance，又依句意爲與現在
   事實相反的假設語氣，故 won't 須改爲 wouldn't；句尾應寫出
   and let go of her hand。

   → If I had a second chance, I wouldn't make the same
     mistake and let go of her hand. 【正】

   【註釋】 ex-girlfriend (ˈɛksˈgɝlfrɛnd) *n.* 前女友
   joyfully (ˈdʒɔɪfəlɪ) *adv.* 愉快地
   ugly (ˈʌglɪ) *adj.* 醜的　　guy (gaɪ) *n.* 人；傢伙
   show (ʃo) *v.* 表示　　hand (hænd) *v.* 拿給
   Dear John letter 分手信
   attention (əˈtɛnʃən) *n.* 注意 (力)
   split up with sb. 和某人分手 (= *break up with sb.*)
   a second 另一個　　*let go of* 放開

TEST 68

If you have extra stuff on your hands, don't forget online garage sales! 1. 你不要的物品可能可以在網路上被變成現金。 You can sell a wide range of things online, ranging from computers to antiques. Neither buying nor selling online is difficult. First, users pay a fee to list their goods. Then, buyers bid on the item. 2. 當拍賣結束時，出價最高的人得標。 The seller is responsible for the shipment. After the sale, the buyer and seller can post comments about the sale on each other's profile.

Sounds appealing, doesn't it? Why not go ahead and begin browsing. You might find something you could use and make your money stretch with these "online garage sales."

1. ....

2. ....

TEST 68 詳解

1. *Things you don't want may become money on the Internet.*【誤】

（北一女中 于恩庭同學）

* become 須改為 be turned into，且 money 須改為 cash（現金）。

→ Your unwanted items may be turned into cash online.【正】
或 You can turn the things you don't need into money online.【正】

2. *At the end of the sale, the person who provides the highest price will get the target.*【誤】（北一女中 于恩庭同學）

* sale 應改成 auction（拍賣），而 provides（提供）應改成 offers「出（價）」，且「得標」是指得到商品，故 target 須改為 item 或 product。

→ When the auction $\begin{Bmatrix} \text{closes,} \\ \text{is over,} \end{Bmatrix}$ the $\begin{Bmatrix} \text{highest bidder} \\ \text{one who bid the most} \end{Bmatrix} \begin{Bmatrix} \text{wins.} \\ \text{gets the item.} \end{Bmatrix}$【正】

【註釋】 extra〔'ɛkstrə〕 *adj.* 額外的；多餘的　　stuff〔stʌf〕 *n.* 東西

online〔'ɑn,laɪn〕 *adj.* 網路上的　　*adv.* 在網路上

garage sale　（在車庫中進行的）清倉大拍賣

a wide range of 很多各式各樣的

range from A *to* B　（範圍）從 A 到 B 都有

antique〔æn'tik〕 *n.* 古董　　fee〔fi〕 *n.* 費用

list〔lɪst〕 *v.* 列出　　goods〔gʊdz〕 *n. pl.* 商品

bid on 投標爭取　　*be responsible for* 負責

shipment〔'ʃɪpmənt〕 *n.* 運送　　post〔post〕 *v.* 張貼

comment〔'kɑmɛnt〕 *n.* 評論　　profile〔'profaɪl〕 *n.* 個人簡介

appealing〔ə'pilɪŋ〕 *adj.* 吸引人的　　browse〔brauz〕 *v.* 瀏覽

stretch〔strɛtʃ〕 *v.* 節儉地延長使用　　item〔'aɪtəm〕 *n.* 物品

cash〔kæʃ〕 *n.* 現金　　bidder〔'bɪdə〕 *n.* 投標者

TEST 69

說明：下面一段短文中，有數處係以中文呈現，請利用上下
文線索（如單字、片語等）將其譯成正確、通順、達
意且前後連貫的英文。

My father was a struggling lawyer, but I always knew he was special. 1. 他不是用批評的，而是用讚美來使我們發揮最好的潛能。 He has also always been very understanding. At the age of 15, I started a magazine. It was taking up a great amount of my time. I decided to leave school. 2. 了解到我已經下定決心，我父親就鼓勵我追求自己的夢想。 As it turned out, my little magazine went on to become a national magazine for young people in the U.K. I owe what I have to his love and encouragement.

1. ....

2. ....

TEST 69 詳解

1. *Instead of criticizing, he praised to make us show our best potential.* 【誤】

   * to make us show...potential 須改成 to bring out our best 或
   to encourage us to reach our potential。

   → $\left.\begin{array}{l} \text{Instead of} \\ \text{Rather than} \end{array}\right\}$ criticizing, he used praise to

   $\left\{\begin{array}{l} \text{bring out our best.} \\ \text{encourage us to do our best.} \end{array}\right.$ 【正】

2. *Understand I had made up my mind, my father encouraged me to pursue my own dream.* 【誤】

   * 須將 Understand 改成 Understanding。

   → $\left.\begin{array}{l} \text{Realizing} \\ \text{Knowing} \end{array}\right\}$ that I had made up my mind, my father

   encouraged me to $\left\{\begin{array}{l} \text{pursue} \\ \text{go after} \\ \text{follow} \end{array}\right\}$ my dream. 【正】

【註釋】 struggling〔'strʌglɪŋ〕*adj.* 必須努力奮鬥才能謀生的
   understanding〔͵ʌndə'stændɪŋ〕*adj.* 明理的；體諒的
   start〔stɑrt〕*v.* 創辦   **take up** 佔用
   a great amount of 大量的   **turn out** 結果
   go on to V. 接著就~   **the U.K.** 英國 (= *the United Kingdom*)
   owe...to ~ 把…歸功於~
   encouragement〔ɪn'kɝɪdʒmənt〕*n.* 鼓勵
   instead of⋯ 不⋯而~ (= *rather than*)
   criticize〔'krɪtə͵saɪz〕*v.* 批評
   reach *one's* **potential** 發揮潛力 (= *achieve one's potential*)

TEST 70

說明：下面一段短文中，有數處係以中文呈現，請利用上下文線索（如單字、片語等）將其譯成正確、通順、達意且前後連貫的英文。

Angkor Wat was built in the 12th century by the Khmers, and they founded an empire that once ruled over Cambodia. 1.雖然它很荒涼，這座寺廟仍然看起來很雄偉。 Huge stone towers rose out of the silent jungle. Far away, by the end of the long stone-paved road lay the temple. The stairs to the temple were very steep. The walls inside the temple were covered with images. There were many elephants and snakes carved into the walls. 2.對發現這些遺跡的探險家而言，當時一定是多麼的神奇啊！ The Khmers had created a golden, now long lost, civilization.

1. ....

2. ....

TEST 70 詳解

1. *Although it is bleak, this temple still looks magnificent.* 【誤】

（和平高中 曹家豪同學）

* 依句意爲過去式，故 is 須改爲 was，且 looks 須改爲 looked。

→ Deserted as it was,
  Although it was abandoned, ⎫ the temple still

  looked ⎰ majestic.
  ⎱ magnificent. 【正】

2. *As for these adventuror who found traces, how miracle it was that time!* 【誤】 （和平高中 曹家豪同學）

*「探險家」是 explorer，而不是 adventurer（冒險家）；how miracle…time 須改爲 how miraculous it was at that time。

→ How magical it must have been for the explorers who discovered these ruins! 【正】

【註釋】 Angkor Wat（ˈæŋkɔrˈwɑt）n. 吳哥窟
　　　　Khmer（kmɛr）n. 高棉人　　found（faʊnd）v. 建立
　　　　empire（ˈɛmpaɪr）n. 帝國　　*rule over* 統治
　　　　Cambodia（kæmˈbodɪə）n. 柬埔寨　　tower（taʊɚ）n. 塔
　　　　rise out of 高聳於　　jungle（ˈdʒʌŋgḷ）n. 叢林
　　　　stone-paved（ˈstonˌpevd）adj. 石頭鋪的　　lie（laɪ）v. 位於
　　　　temple（ˈtɛmpḷ）n. 寺廟　　stair（stɛr）n. 階梯；樓梯
　　　　steep（stip）adj. 陡峭的　　image（ˈɪmɪdʒ）n. 圖像
　　　　snake（snek）n. 蛇　　carve（kɑrv）v. 雕刻
　　　　lost（lɔst）adj. 消失的　　civilization（ˌsɪvḷaɪˈzeʃən）n. 文明
　　　　bleak（blik）adj. 荒涼的　　deserted（dɪˈzɝtɪd）adj. 荒涼的
　　　　abandoned（əˈbændənd）adj. 荒涼的
　　　　majestic（məˈdʒɛstɪk）adj. 雄偉的
　　　　magnificent（mægˈnɪfəsṇt）adj. 壯麗的
　　　　explorer（ɪkˈsplorɚ）n. 探險家　　ruins（ˈruɪnz）n. pl. 遺跡

TEST 71

說明：下面一段短文中，有數處係以中文呈現，請利用上下文線索（如單字、片語等）將其譯成正確、通順、達意且前後連貫的英文。

Fixed stars made up of small pieces of matter are the largest bodies in the universe. The sun is the closest star to the earth, with a surface temperature about 6,000 degrees centigrade. Most of the stars we see are hotter than the sun, but because they are far away from the earth, 1. 我們只把它們看作是在空中的小光點。 In the daytime, due to the sunlight, the stars are invisible to us. The stars seem to twinkle when the sky gets dark. As a matter of fact, 2. 閃爍不是由星星本身造成的，而是由地球的大氣層造成的。 Each layer of the earth's atmosphere has its temperature, density and speed of air movement. As the light of a distant star goes through the layers, it gets distorted and this makes the star twinkle.

1. ....

2. ....

TEST 71 詳解

1. <u>*we only see them as small light points in the air.*</u>【誤】

   * small light points 須改成 small points of light，且 in the air 須改成 in the sky。

   → we only see them as $\begin{Bmatrix} \text{tiny} \\ \text{very small} \end{Bmatrix}$ $\begin{Bmatrix} \text{dots} \\ \text{points} \end{Bmatrix}$

   of light in the sky.【正】

2. <u>*glimmer doesn't result from the stars itself, but results from the earth atmosphere.*</u>【誤】

   * glimmer 之前，須加 the；itself 須改成 themselves，且 earth 須改成 earth's。

   → the twinkling isn't caused by the stars themselves, but by the earth's atmosphere.【正】

【註釋】 fixed〔fɪkst〕*adj.* 固定的　　***be made up of*** 由…組成
　　　　matter〔'mætɚ〕*n.* 物質　　body〔'bɑdɪ〕*n.* (天) 體
　　　　universe〔'junə,vɝs〕*n.* 宇宙　　star〔stɑr〕*n.* 恆星
　　　　surface〔'sɝfɪs〕*adj.* 表面的
　　　　centigrade〔'sɛntə,gred〕*adj.* 攝氏的
　　　　in the daytime 在白天　　***due to*** 由於
　　　　invisible〔ɪn'vɪzəbḷ〕*adj.* 看不見的
　　　　twinkle〔'twɪŋkḷ〕*v.* 閃爍　　***as a matter of fact*** 事實上
　　　　layer〔'leɚ〕*n.* 層　　atmosphere〔'ætməs,fɪr〕*n.* 大氣層
　　　　density〔'dɛnsətɪ〕*n.* 密度　　movement〔'muvmənt〕*n.* 移動
　　　　distant〔'dɪstənt〕*adj.* 遙遠的
　　　　distorted〔dɪs'tɔrtɪd〕*adj.* 扭曲的　　tiny〔'taɪnɪ〕*adj.* 微小的

TEST 72

Tom tried to behave badly in class so that the teacher would punish him. His wish granted, Tom was made to sit on the girls' side of the classroom. His purpose was to be able to sit near Becky, the girl he liked. When he tried to please Becky with different gestures, the teacher noticed his tricks. Just when Tom was enjoying making Becky laugh and was smiling happily at Becky, 1. 他感覺到老師抓著他的耳朵，並且他就被拉離開座位。 The teacher dragged him across the classroom and set him down in his own seat. She stood over him angrily for a few long moments and then moved away to the front of the classroom without saying a word. 2. 儘管他的耳朵痛，但湯姆的心卻充滿了喜悅。 He knew that he had fallen in love — sweet puppy love.

1. ....

2. ....

TEST 72 詳解

1. *he felt the teacher grasp his ears, and pulled away from seats.* 【誤】（陽明高中 鄭筱彤同學）

   * ears 應改成 ear；and pulled 須改成 and he was pulled，且 seats 須改成 the seat。

   → he felt the teacher seize his ear, and he was

   $\left\{ \begin{array}{l} \text{pulled} \\ \text{dragged} \end{array} \right\}$ off the seat. 【正】

2. *Despite of his ears ache, Tom's heart is filled with joy.* 【誤】

   （陽明高中 鄭筱彤同學）

   * Despite 後不加 of，故須將 of 去掉，又 despite 是介系詞，故 his ears ache 須改成 his painful ear，又依句意為過去式，故 is 須改為 was。

   → $\left. \begin{array}{l} \text{Despite his painful ear,} \\ \text{Even though he had a pain in his ear,} \end{array} \right\}$

   Tom's heart was full of joy. 【正】

   【註釋】 behave〔bɪ'hev〕v. 行為舉止　　*so that* 以便於
   grant〔grænt〕v. 應允　　please〔pliz〕v. 取悅
   gesture〔'dʒɛstʃɚ〕n. 姿勢；手勢
   trick〔trɪk〕n. 把戲
   drag〔dræg〕v. 拖　　set〔sɛt〕v. 安置
   stand over 監督；注視　　*fall in love* 戀愛
   puppy love 初戀　　seize〔siz〕v. 抓住
   painful〔'penfəl〕adj. 疼痛的　　*be full of* 充滿了

TEST 73

With over two billion novels sold, 1. Agatha Christie 被認為是僅次於莎士比亞，全世界第二暢銷的作家。 She was one of the first women to write murder mysteries. *The Mousetrap*, holds the record for the longest-running stage play of all time. She enjoyed challenging the reader to work out who the murderer was before the answer was revealed. She also played fair, 2. 確定有提供足夠的線索來解開謎團。 She was also the first to write murder mysteries that took place in secluded places and involved a group of suspects.

1. ....

2. ....

TEST 73 詳解

1. *Agatha Christie is considered to be the second best-selling writer just inferior to...* 【誤】（師大附中 劉冠麟同學）

   * just inferior to...須改成 , second only to Shakespeare。

   → Agatha Christie is $\begin{Bmatrix} \text{considered to be} \\ \text{recognized as} \end{Bmatrix}$

   $\begin{Bmatrix} \text{the world's second-best-selling author after} \\ \text{one of the world's best-selling writers, second} \end{Bmatrix}$

   $\begin{Bmatrix} \text{Shakespeare.} \\ \text{only to Shakespeare.} \end{Bmatrix}$ 【正】

2. *making sure to provide enough cule to solve the mistery.* 【誤】

   （師大附中 劉冠麟同學）

   * cule 須改成 clues（線索）；mistery 須改成 mystery（謎）。

   → making sure that enough clues were given to solve

   the $\begin{Bmatrix} \text{puzzle.} \\ \text{mystery.} \end{Bmatrix}$ 【正】

【註釋】 billion〔ˈbɪljən〕n. 十億
mystery（ˈmɪstrɪ）n. 推理小說；神祕小說；謎
mousetrap（ˈmaʊsˌtræp）n. 捕鼠器
hold the record 保持紀錄　　run〔rʌn〕v.（戲劇）連續上演
stage play 舞台劇　　**of all time** 從古至今
challenge（ˈtʃælɪndʒ）v. 向…挑戰；要求　　**work out** 想出
reveal〔rɪˈvil〕v. 透露　　**play fair** 光明正大地行動
secluded〔sɪˈkludɪd〕adj. 隔離的　　involve〔ɪnˈvɑlv〕v. 牽涉
suspect（ˈsʌspɛkt）n. 嫌疑犯　　clue〔klu〕n. 線索
solve〔sɑlv〕v. 解決　　puzzle（ˈpʌzḷ）n. 謎

TEST 74

說明：下面一段短文中，有數處係以中文呈現，請利用上下文線索（如單字、片語等）將其譯成正確、通順、達意且前後連貫的英文。

Throughout the ages, people have always looked up at the stars in the night sky, wondering about them. <u>1. 他們用不同的方式，來記錄對天空的觀察結果。</u> The ancient Greeks, for example, picked out groups of bright stars that looked like pictures of animals and people.

There are billions of stars in our galaxy. <u>2. 天文學家用光年來測量星星之間的距離，</u> because light has the fastest speed of anything in the universe. It travels at a speed of 186,000 miles per second, or about 6 trillion miles per year.

1. ....

2. ....

TEST 74 詳解

1. *They use different ways to record the sky observations.* 【誤】

   * the sky observations 應改成 the observations of the sky。

   → They $\left\{\begin{array}{l}\text{recorded}\\\text{kept track of}\end{array}\right\}$ $\left\{\begin{array}{l}\text{their observations of}\\\text{what they saw in}\end{array}\right\}$

   the sky in $\left\{\begin{array}{l}\text{different}\\\text{a variety of}\end{array}\right\}$ ways. 【正】

2. *Astronomers use "lightyear" to measure the distance between stars and stars,* 【誤】

   * "lightyear" 應改成 light year (光年)，且 between stars and stars
   應改成 between stars。

   → Astronomers $\left\{\begin{array}{l}\text{measure}\\\text{calculate}\end{array}\right\}$ $\left\{\begin{array}{l}\text{the distances between}\\\text{how far apart the}\end{array}\right\}$

   $\left.\begin{array}{l}\text{the stars}\\\text{stars are}\end{array}\right\}$ in light years, 【正】

【註釋】 throughout〔θru'aʊt〕*prep.* 遍及　　age〔edʒ〕*n.* 時代
　　　　ancient〔'enʃənt〕*adj.* 古代的　　***pick out*** 挑選出
　　　　billion〔'bɪljən〕*n.* 十億　　galaxy〔'gæləksɪ〕*n.* 銀河系
　　　　universe〔'junə,vɝs〕*n.* 宇宙　　travel〔'trævl̩〕*v.* 行進
　　　　per〔pɝ〕*prep.* 每…　　second〔'sɛkənd〕*n.* 秒
　　　　observation〔,ɑbzɚ'veʃən〕*n.* 觀察
　　　　astronomer〔ə'strɑnəmɚ〕*n.* 天文學家
　　　　light year 光年

TEST 75

We often envy rich people and believe they can buy anything they want with money. 1. <u>然而，仍然有很多東西是用金錢買不到的。</u> For example, money can't buy peace of mind, from which comes a healthy view of life. 2. <u>錢可以買到奉承，但它卻買不到真正的友誼。</u> In fact, the things that money can't buy would make a long list. So it is good to check and make sure we haven't lost the valuable things life has to offer.

1. ....

2. ....

TEST 75 詳解

1. *However, there are lots of things that can't be bought by*
   bill.【誤】（延平高中 王家逸同學）

   * there are 後面須加上 still，並將 by bill 改成 with money。

   → However,
     But ⟩ there are still many things that can't

   be bought with money. 【正】

2. *Money can buy pleasant, but it can't buy the real friendship.*【誤】

   （延平高中 王家逸同學）

   * 須將 pleasant（令人愉快的）改成 flattery（奉承），並將 the 去掉。

   → Money can buy flattery, but it can't buy real
     friendship. 【正】

   【註釋】 envy (ˈɛnvɪ) v. 羨慕　　peace (pis) n. 平靜
   　　　　healthy (ˈhɛlθɪ) adj. 健康的
   　　　　view of life 人生觀 (= *outlook on life* = *philosophy of life*)
   　　　　check (tʃɛk) v. 檢查　　*make sure* 確定
   　　　　valuable (ˈvæljʊəbḷ) adj. 珍貴的
   　　　　life has to offer 人生所能提供的
   　　　　flattery (ˈflætərɪ) n. 恭維；奉承

TEST 76

説明：下面一段短文中，有數處係以中文呈現，請利用上下文線索（如單字、片語等）將其譯成正確、通順、達意且前後連貫的英文。

The famous Greek writer Nikos Kazantzakis pointed out that a good teacher acts as a bridge over which students can cross toward understanding. 1. 一旦學生們學會所教的課程，他們就能跨越這座橋，並且製造自己的新橋。 They should be able to think and live independently. His idea comes close to an old saying: "Give a man a fish; you have fed him for today. Teach a man to fish; you have fed him for a lifetime." It is true that a good teacher should teach students life skills. And when they master these skills, 2. 無論學生遭遇到什麼困難，他們都將能夠生存。

1. ....

2. ....

TEST 76 詳解

1. <u>*Once the students learned the course, they could go across*</u>
   <u>*the bridge and produce their own bridge.*</u>【誤】(建國中學 周芳睿同學)

   * 依句意為現在式，故 learned 須改為 learn，could 須改為 can；
   course 後面須加上 being taught，而 their own bridge 須改為
   their own new bridge。

   → Once they learn the lessons being taught,

   students can $\begin{cases} \text{cross} \\ \text{go over} \end{cases}$ the bridge and $\begin{cases} \text{make} \\ \text{construct} \end{cases}$

   new bridges of their own. 【正】

2. <u>*whatever difficulties the students faced with, they could*</u>
   <u>*survive.*</u>【誤】(建國中學 周芳睿同學)

   * faced with 須改為 face，而 could 須改為 can。

   → students will be able to survive no matter what

   $\begin{cases} \text{difficulty} \\ \text{trouble} \end{cases}$ they $\begin{cases} \text{may get into.} \\ \text{face.} \end{cases}$ 【正】

【註釋】 ***point out*** 指出   ***act as*** 充當
   independently〔͵ɪndɪˈpɛndəntlɪ〕*adv.* 獨立地
   come close to 接近   saying〔ˈseɪŋ〕*n.* 格言
   lifetime〔ˈlaɪf͵taɪm〕*n.* 一生
   master〔ˈmæstɚ〕*v.* 精通
   survive〔səˈvaɪv〕*v.* 生存；存活   ***get into*** 陷入

TEST 77

Rolls-Royce cars and Steinway pianos help to define "excellence". These companies make a commitment to the highest standards of quality regardless of time or cost. 1.他們注意每個細節，並且與品質有關的地方，都絕不妥協。 For example, all 12,000 parts of a Steinway piano are installed by hand, and each piano takes a year to complete. 2.因為它們高水準的工藝，所以大多數音樂會的鋼琴家都會偏愛它們。 Unlike cars in the early 1900s, which ran poorly, Rolls-Royce cars run so smoothly that they hardly make a noise. No wonder that even after a hundred years, Rolls-Royce cars and Steinway pianos still enjoy a reputation for excellence.

1. ....

2. ....

TEST 77 詳解

1. *They focus on every detail and never comprise anything related to quality.* 【誤】

   * 須將 comprise（組成）改爲 compromise（妥協）。

   → They pay attention to every detail, and make no compromise where quality is concerned. 【正】

2. *Due to their first-rate craft, most of the concert pianists prefer them.* 【誤】

   * 須將 craft（技能）改成 craftsmanship（工藝）。

   → Because of their high level of craftsmanship, most concert pianists $\left\{ \begin{array}{l} \text{have a preference for} \\ \text{prefer} \end{array} \right\}$ them. 【正】

【註釋】 Rolls-Royce〔'rols'rɔɪs〕 n. 勞斯萊斯
define〔dɪ'faɪn〕v. 替…下定義
excellence〔'ɛksḷəns〕n. 卓越；優秀
commitment〔kə'mɪtmənt〕n. 承諾；專心致力 < to >
make a commitment to 致力於
regardless of 不管；不論；不分
install〔ɪn'stɔl〕v. 安裝   run〔rʌn〕v. 行駛
smoothly〔'smuðlɪ〕adv. 平滑地；流暢地
enjoy〔ɪn'dʒɔɪ〕v. 享有
reputation〔ˌrɛpjə'teʃən〕n. 聲譽
focus on 專注於   ***pay attention to*** 注意
compromise〔'kɑmprəˌmaɪz〕v. n. 妥協

TEST 78

說明：下面一段短文中，有數處係以中文呈現，請利用上下文線索（如單字、片語等）將其譯成正確、通順、達意且前後連貫的英文。

"To Electra" is apparently a love poem. 1.我們可以感受到這位詩人有多想要親吻 Electra。 He dare not ask her for a kiss, nor dare he beg a smile.

However, he is content to kiss the air that has just received Electra's breath. So perhaps he should just love her from a distance — a secret love kept to himself. 2.這種愛是非常純粹而且天真，不是嗎？ Have you ever felt this way about someone you were attracted to?

1. ....

2. ....

TEST 78 詳解

1. *We can feel how the poeter wants to kiss Electra.* 【誤】

(建國中學 鍾秉軒同學)

* how 須改為 how much，而 poeter 須改為 poet (詩人)。

→ We can $\begin{Bmatrix} \text{feel} \\ \text{sense} \end{Bmatrix}$ how much the poet $\begin{Bmatrix} \text{would like} \\ \text{wants} \end{Bmatrix}$

to kiss Electra. 【正】

2. *This kind of love is pretty sheer and naive, isn't it?* 【誤】

(建國中學 鍾秉軒同學)

* sheer (全然的) 應改為 pure (純粹的)。

→ This $\begin{Bmatrix} \text{kind} \\ \text{type} \end{Bmatrix}$ of love is $\begin{Bmatrix} \text{so} \\ \text{very} \end{Bmatrix}$ pure and innocent,

isn't it? 【正】

【註釋】 apparently〔əˈpɛrəntlɪ〕*adv.* 顯然

dare〔dɛr〕*aux.* 敢　　beg〔bɛg〕*v.* 乞求

content〔kənˈtɛnt〕*adj.* 滿足的

breath〔brɛθ〕*n.* 呼吸　　distance〔ˈdɪstəns〕*n.* 距離

be attracted to 被…吸引　　sense〔sɛns〕*v.* 感覺

poet〔ˈpo·ɪt〕*n.* 詩人　　pure〔pjʊr〕*adj.* 純粹的

innocent〔ˈɪnəsn̩t〕*adj.* 天真的

TEST 79

Experts have made many interesting conclusions about self-esteem that are worthy of note. First, we get a large part of our self-esteem from our family, especially in our younger years. <u>1.當父母有高度的自尊心時，他們通常會將這個特質遺傳給他們的子女。</u> Second, when we feel good about ourselves, we are much less likely to harm ourselves. This includes developing drug and alcohol problems or even committing crimes. Finally, remember no one is born with self-esteem — <u>2.它是必須藉由努力工作以及積極的態度才能培養出來的。</u>

1. ....

2. ....

TEST 79　詳解

1. <u>*When parents have high self-esteem, they usually inherit this*</u> <u>*characteristic to their kids.*</u>【誤】（建國中學 曹育彰同學）

* inherit（繼承）應改為 pass on「將…傳（給）」。

→ When parents have $\begin{cases} \text{high self-esteem,} \\ \text{respect for themselves,} \end{cases}$ they

usually pass this $\begin{cases} \text{quality} \\ \text{trait} \end{cases}$ on to their children.【正】

2. *it must be developed by hard working and positive attitude.*【誤】

（建國中學 曹育彰同學）

* by hard working 可改成 through hard work，而 attitude 為可數名詞，故須改成 a positive attitude。

→ it is something that must be $\begin{cases} \text{developed} \\ \text{built up} \end{cases}$ through

$\begin{cases} \text{effort} \\ \text{hard work} \end{cases}$ and a positive attitude.【正】

【註釋】　expert（ˈɛkspɝt）n. 專家
　　　　　conclusion（kənˈkluʒən）n. 結論
　　　　　self-esteem（ˌsɛlfəˈstim）n. 自尊心
　　　　　be worthy of 值得　　note（not）n. 注意
　　　　　feel good about 對…感到滿意
　　　　　include（ɪnˈklud）v. 包括　　develop（dɪˈvɛləp）v. 培養
　　　　　drug（drʌg）n. 毒品　　alcohol（ˈælkəˌhɔl）n. 酒精
　　　　　commit a crime 犯罪　　*pass～on to* 將～傳給…
　　　　　hard work 努力（= *effort*）　　positive（ˈpɑzətɪv）adj. 積極的

TEST 80

> 説明：下面一段短文中，有數處係以中文呈現，請利用上下文線索（如單字、片語等）將其譯成正確、通順、達意且前後連貫的英文。

Yo-Yo Ma, a world-famous cellist, does not limit himself to playing classical music. In addition to American country music, 1.他演奏住在非洲沙漠裡及中國古代絲路的人的音樂。 In fact, Ma's music consists of so great a diversity of styles that we are able to appreciate various music styles just by listening to him.

Ma says he feels lucky to have grown up in a Chinese family 2.因為大多數的中國父母都期待自己的小孩受良好的教育並且很有禮貌。 Despite the fact that his father was quite strict at times, Ma was left free to discover his own special interests and abilities, which led to his great achievements in later years.

1. _____

2. _____

TEST 80 詳解

1. <u>he play the music of people which live in African desert and Chinese ancient silk-road.</u> 【誤】 (延平高中 黃楷婷同學)

   * play 須改成 plays；which 須改成 who，而 desert 為可數名詞，須改成 deserts；silk-road 須改成 Silk Road。

   → he plays the music of people living in

   $\left\{ \begin{array}{l} \text{the deserts of Africa} \\ \text{African deserts} \end{array} \right\}$ and the music of China's

   ancient Silk Road. 【正】

2. <u>because almost all Chinese parents expect their own children can accept good education and be polite.</u> 【誤】 (延平高中 黃楷婷同學)

   * expect 接受詞後，須加不定詞，故 can accept good education and be polite 須改成 to be well-educated and polite。

   → because most Chinese parents expect their children to

   become well-educated and $\left\{ \begin{array}{l} \text{well-mannered.} \\ \text{polite.} \end{array} \right.$ 【正】

【註釋】 cellist (ˈtʃɛlɪst) n. 大提琴家
classical (ˈklæsɪkḷ) adj. 古典的
in addition to 除了　*consist of* 由…組成；包含
a diversity of 各種不同的　appreciate (əˈpriʃɪ,et) v. 欣賞
strict (strɪkt) adj. 嚴格的　*at times* 有時候
leave (liv) v. 任由　*lead to* 導致
achievements (əˈtʃivmənts) n. pl. 成就
desert (ˈdɛzɚt) n. 沙漠
ancient (ˈenʃənt) adj. 古代的　*Silk Road* 絲路
well-mannered (ˈwɛlˈmænɚd) adj. 有禮貌的

TEST 81

說明：下面一段短文中，有數處係以中文呈現，請利用上下文線索（如單字、片語等）將其譯成正確、通順、達意且前後連貫的英文。

One day when I was about to get off the bus, I couldn't find my EasyCard, nor could I find any money in my pockets. 1. 我站在公車前門的旁邊，覺得我的臉頰變得越來越熱。 Just at that embarrassing moment a girl in my school's uniform came to my assistance and paid the bus fare for me. That was how I met my best friend in high school, Carol.

From then on, we took the same bus home. 2. 我以前自己搭公車時，常會聽 MP3。 Now we chat happily about what happened during the day. We talk like friends who have known each other all their lives though we met just a month ago. I hope our friendship can last forever.

1. ....

2. ....

TEST 81 詳解

1. *I stood by the front door of the bus, and felt my check became hotter and hotter.* 【誤】（成功高中 李佳穎同學）

  * check 應改為 cheeks，且 felt 為感官動詞，接受詞之後，須接原形
    動詞，故 became 須改成 become。

  → I stood by the front door of the bus, feeling my
     cheeks growing hotter and hotter. 【正】

2. *I used to listen to MP3 when I took bus before.* 【誤】

  （成功高中 李佳穎同學）

  * MP3 須改為 my MP3，而 used to 就是指「以前」，故句尾的
    before 要去掉，以免重複，然後加上 by myself。

  → $\left.\begin{array}{l}\text{I used to listen to}\\ \text{Before, I listened to}\end{array}\right\}$ my MP3 when I $\left\{\begin{array}{l}\text{rode}\\ \text{was}\end{array}\right\}$

   on the bus $\left\{\begin{array}{l}\text{by myself.}\\ \text{alone.}\end{array}\right.$ 【正】

【註釋】 ***be about to V.*** 正要～   ***get off*** 下（車）
    pocket〔'pɑkɪt〕*n.* 口袋
    embarrassing〔ɪm'bærəsɪŋ〕*adj.* 令人尷尬的
    uniform〔'junə,fɔrm〕*n.* 制服
    come to one's ***assistance*** 來幫助某人（= come to one's aid）
    fare〔fɛr〕*n.* 車資   ***from then on*** 從那時起
    chat〔tʃæt〕*v.* 聊天   ***all*** one's ***life*** 一輩子
    last〔læst〕*v.* 持續   cheek〔tʃik〕*n.* 臉頰
    grow〔gro〕*v.* 變得   ***used to V.*** 以前～
    by oneself 獨自

TEST 82

說明：下面一段短文中，有數處係以中文呈現，請利用上下
　　　文線索（如單字、片語等）將其譯成正確、通順、達
　　　意且前後連貫的英文。

In the 1940s, an employee at an American department store created a character to sell more goods at Christmas time. The new character was a red-nosed reindeer, Rudolph. In the man's story, <u>1. 其他的馴鹿因為 Rudolph 有大的紅鼻子而看不起牠。</u> All of them used to laugh and call him names. They never let poor Rudolph join in any reindeer games. Rudolph found himself not fully accepted by the other reindeer. One Christmas Eve, however, it seemed that Santa Claus had nothing to guide his sleigh on his travels around the world. <u>2. 突然間，聖誕老公公想到 Rudolph 和牠明亮、發光的鼻子，所以就要求 Rudolph 帶路。</u> As a result, Santa's gifts were delivered on time. Children woke up on Christmas morning and found their stockings filled with candy and toys.

1. ....

2. ....

TEST 82 詳解

1. *because Rudolph has a big red nose, another deer contempt him.*【誤】（成淵高中 黃信和同學）

   * 依句意為過去式，故 has 須改為 had，且 another deer 須改成 the other reindeer；contempt（輕視）是名詞，須改成 despised（輕視）。

   → the other reindeer looked down on Rudolph

   $\left\{ \begin{array}{l} \text{because of his} \\ \text{because he had a} \end{array} \right\}$ big red nose.【正】

2. *Suddenly, Santa Claus thinks of Rudolph and his bright nose, so he requested Rudolph to lead the road.*【誤】（成淵高中 黃信和同學）

   * thinks 須改成 thought，又 bright 須改成 bright, shiny，且 lead the road 須改成 lead the way（帶路）。

   → $\left. \begin{array}{l} \text{All at once,} \\ \text{Suddenly,} \end{array} \right\}$ Santa thought of Rudolph and his

   bright, shiny nose, and $\left\{ \begin{array}{l} \text{Rudolph was asked} \\ \text{he asked Rudolph} \end{array} \right\}$

   to lead the way.【正】

【註釋】 employee〔͵ɛmplɔɪˋi〕*n.* 員工　　character〔ˋkærɪktɚ〕*n.* 人物
　　　　goods〔gʊdz〕*n. pl.* 商品　　reindeer〔ˋrendɪr〕*n.* 馴鹿
　　　　used to 以前　　***call sb. names*** 辱罵某人
　　　　guide〔gaɪd〕*v.* 引導　　sleigh〔sle〕*n.* 雪車
　　　　as a result 因此　　***on time*** 準時　　***wake up*** 醒來
　　　　stockings〔ˋstɑkɪŋz〕*n. pl.* 長襪　　***be filled with*** 裝滿了
　　　　look down upon 輕視；看不起（= *despise*）
　　　　all at once 突然間　　shiny〔ˋʃaɪnɪ〕*adj.* 閃亮的
　　　　lead the way 帶路

TEST 83

A life without dreams is like a boat without direction. 1. <u>爲了實現自我，你應該知道自己的夢想是什麼。</u> You may find this effortless if you are very talented in certain areas. However, you may have a hard time finding one if you are just as common as everybody else. In this case, drawing inspiration from great people or even people in your daily life may shed some light on what you'd like to be in the future. In addition, listening to the little voice from within also helps you understand yourself. 2. <u>無論你的夢想是否偉大，它都是很有價值的。</u> As long as you have a clear idea of what your dream is, you can be sure that you won't waste your life drifting away like an aimless boat.

1. ....

2. ....

TEST 83 詳解

1. _For the purpose of fulfilling yourself, you should know what
   is your dream._ 【誤】(建國中學 鄭維同學)

   * what is your dream 應改成名詞子句 what your dream is。

   → To fulfill yourself, you should know what your
      dream is. 【正】

2. _No matter your dream is great or not, it's valuable._ 【誤】

   (建國中學 鄭維同學)

   * 須在 No matter 之後加上 whether。

   → Whether your dream is $\begin{cases} \text{grand or not,} \\ \text{big or small,} \end{cases}$

   it is $\begin{cases} \text{of great value.} \\ \text{valuable.} \end{cases}$ 【正】

【註釋】 find〔faɪnd〕v. 覺得　　effortless〔'ɛfətlɪs〕adj. 不費力的
　　　　 talented〔'tæləntɪd〕adj. 有才能的
　　　　 certain〔'sɝtn̩〕adj. 某些　　area〔'ɛrɪə〕n. 領域
　　　　 have a hard time + _V-ing_ 很難~
　　　　 case〔kes〕n. 情況　　draw〔drɔ〕v. 獲得
　　　　 inspiration〔ˌɪnspə'reʃən〕n. 靈感
　　　　 daily〔'delɪ〕adj. 日常的
　　　　 shed light on 使人了解某事；使某事顯得非常清楚
　　　　 within〔wɪð'ɪn〕n. 內部　　_drift away_ 漸漸離開
　　　　 aimless〔'emlɪs〕adj. 無目標的
　　　　 fulfill oneself 實現自我；完全發揮自己的潛力
　　　　 grand〔grænd〕adj. 雄偉的；遠大的
　　　　 of value 有價值的 (= _valuable_)

TEST 84

The teacher brought the boy and me to the front of the class. 1. 在她的書桌中間，有個大大、圓圓的物體。 She asked us what color it was. I couldn't believe the boy said the object was white when it was obviously black. The teacher told us to change places, and then she asked me what the color of the object was. I had to answer, "White." It was an object with differently colored sides. My teacher taught me a very important lesson that day. 2. 我們必須站在另一個人的立場，透過他或她的眼睛來看情況。

1. ....

2. ....

TEST 84 詳解

1. *In the middle of her desk surface, there was a big and round*
   object.【誤】（北一女中 傅子耘同學）

   * 須將 surface 去掉，且 a big and round 須改爲 a big round。

   → In the $\left\{\begin{array}{l}\text{middle} \\ \text{center}\end{array}\right\}$ of her desk was a $\left\{\begin{array}{l}\text{large} \\ \text{big}\end{array}\right\}$

   round $\left\{\begin{array}{l}\text{object.} \\ \text{thing.}\end{array}\right\}$【正】

2. *We should stand on another person's position looking the*
   situation through his or her eyes.【誤】（北一女中 傅子耘同學）

   * 須將 stand on another person's position 改爲 stand in the other
   person's shoes 或 put ourselves in the other person's position，
   且 looking 須改爲 and look at。

   → We $\left\{\begin{array}{l}\text{must} \\ \text{have to}\end{array}\right\}$ $\left\{\begin{array}{l}\text{stand in the other person's shoes} \\ \text{put ourselves in the other person's place}\end{array}\right\}$

   and look at $\left\{\begin{array}{l}\text{the situation} \\ \text{things}\end{array}\right\}$ $\left\{\begin{array}{l}\text{through his or her eyes.} \\ \text{from his point of view.}\end{array}\right\}$【正】

【註釋】 object〔'ɑbdʒɪkt〕*n.* 物體
　　　　obviously〔'ɑbvɪəslɪ〕*adv.* 明顯地
　　　　differently colored sides 不同顏色的邊
　　　　lesson〔'lɛsn̩〕*n.* 敎訓　　middle〔'mɪdl̩〕*n.* 中間
　　　　stand in *one's* ***shoes*** 站在某人的立場
　　　　　　(= *put oneself in one's place* = *put oneself in one's position*)
　　　　through〔θru〕*prep.* 透過

TEST 85

On hot summer days, one can easily find a wide selection of ice cream and other ice treats in the frozen foods section in supermarkets, as well as on the streets. 1. 吃冰品似乎是很自然的事，所以沒有人能抗拒。 However, for most of history these delicious treats were not available to everyone. For a very long time, only very rich, powerful people ate these ice treats. For instance, the Roman Emperor Nero used to get runners to run to the mountains to get snow so he could have his ice treat. 2. 現在，很多人喜歡喝冰淇淋汽水，以及吃蛋捲冰淇淋。 What they might not know is that these uses for ice cream were all invented by accident.

1. ....

2. ....

TEST 85 詳解

1. *It's natural that we eating ice product, so no one can resist.* 【誤】（師大附中 邱煒翔同學）

   * that we eating ice product 應改成 to want to eat frozen treats，
   且 resist 須改爲 resist them。

   → Eating ice treats seems to be so natural

   that $\left\{ \begin{array}{l} \text{nobody} \\ \text{no one} \end{array} \right\}$ can resist. 【正】

2. *Many people like to drink ice cream soda and egg roll ice cream now.* 【誤】（師大附中 邱煒翔同學）

   * soda 須改成 sodas，且 and 後面須加動詞 eat；而 egg roll ice cream 須改成 ice cream cones。

   → $\left. \begin{array}{l} \text{Today,} \\ \text{Nowadays,} \end{array} \right\}$ may people like to eat ice cream

   sodas and ice cream cones. 【正】

   【註釋】 *a wide selection of* 很多種類的
   　　　　treat〔trit〕*n.* 非常好的事物　　*ice treat* 冰品
   　　　　frozen〔'frozn̩〕*adj.* 冷凍的　　section〔'sɛkʃən〕*n.* 區域
   　　　　as well as 以及　　*be available to sb.* 是某人可獲得的
   　　　　powerful〔'pauɚfəl〕*adj.* 有權勢的
   　　　　emperor〔'ɛmpərɚ〕*n.* 皇帝
   　　　　Nero〔'niro〕*n.* 尼祿【37-68，羅馬皇帝，迫害基督徒的暴君】
   　　　　used to 以前　　*by accident* 意外地
   　　　　resist〔rɪ'zɪst〕*v.* 抵抗；抗拒　　soda〔'sodə〕*n.* 汽水
   　　　　ice cream cone 蛋捲冰淇淋

TEST 86

說明：下面一段短文中，有數處係以中文呈現，請利用上下
文線索（如單字、片語等）將其譯成正確、通順、達
意且前後連貫的英文。

What is a blog? A blog is everything you can
imagine: a personal diary, a message board, an
information center, etc. In simple terms, a blog is a
web site where you can post things on an ongoing
basis. 1. 無論你想要分享即時的新聞或發表你對政治情況的
評論， it is the right place for you. Besides being an
outlet for you to express yourself, a blog can also be
a perfect place for discussion. If they are moved by
what you write, your readers can leave a message or
e-mail you. Blogs are not just a fad. They are here
to stay. If you haven't started one yet, 2. 你何不連結到
blogger.com 來創造你自己的部落格 and have some fun?

1. ....

2. ....

TEST 86 詳解

1. <u>Whenever you want to share the live news or present your</u>
   <u>comment on the political situations,</u>【誤】（板橋高中 張博雄同學）

   * 須將 Whenever（無論何時）改爲 Whether（無論），並將 live（現場的）
   改爲 recent 或 breaking，且句尾的 situations 須改爲 situation。

   → Whether you want to share $\left\{ \begin{array}{l} \text{breaking} \\ \text{recent} \end{array} \right\}$ news or

   give your $\left\{ \begin{array}{l} \text{comments} \\ \text{opinions} \end{array} \right\}$ on $\left\{ \begin{array}{l} \text{the political situation,} \\ \text{politics,} \end{array} \right.$ 【正】

2. <u>why not you connect to "blogger.com" to create your own blog</u>【誤】

   （板橋高中 張博雄同學）

   * why not you connect 須改爲 why not connect to 或 why don't
   you connect to。

   → why don't you $\left\{ \begin{array}{l} \text{link up to} \\ \text{go to} \end{array} \right\}$ blogger.com

   $\left\{ \begin{array}{l} \text{and} \\ \text{to} \end{array} \right\}$ create $\left\{ \begin{array}{l} \text{your own blog} \\ \text{a blog of your own} \end{array} \right.$ 【正】

【註釋】 blog〔blɑg〕 n. 部落格　　imagine〔ɪˈmædʒɪn〕 v. 想像
diary〔ˈdaɪərɪ〕 n. 日記　　***message board*** 留言板
etc.〔ɛtˈsɛtərə〕等等　　terms〔tɝmz〕 n. pl. 措辭；說法
in simple terms 簡單地說　　***web site*** 網站（= *website*）
post〔post〕 v. 張貼　　ongoing〔ˈɑnˌgoɪŋ〕 adj. 進行中的
on an ongoing basis 持續地　　outlet〔ˈaʊtˌlɛt〕 n. 出口
express〔ɪkˈsprɛs〕 v. 表達　　move〔muv〕 v. 使感動
fad〔fæd〕 n. 一時的流行　　***be here to stay*** 一直存在下去
have fun 玩得愉快　　***breaking news*** 即時新聞
comment〔ˈkɑmɛnt〕 n. 評論　　***link up to*** 連結（= *connect to*）

TEST 87

Bill Gates is a man who enjoys challenges. When young, he was sent to his room and wasn't allowed to go out if he did something wrong. At this time, he let his mind run wild to the outside world. 1.透過他的 "windows"，他已經讓數百萬人能自由地在電腦世界中旅行。 His favorite activity in high school was to play with the only computer in his school. 2.現在他已經變成電腦時代的象徵。 All of this was achieved while he was in his forties.

1. ....

2. ....

TEST 87 詳解

1. *Through his "windows", he had maken billions of people to freely travel in the world of computer.* 【誤】（景美女中 賴華沂同學）

   * had maken 須改為 has enabled，而 billions（數十億）須改為 millions（數百萬），且句尾的 computer 須改為 computers。

   → Through his "windows", he has

$$\left\{ \begin{array}{l} \text{made it possible for} \\ \text{enabled} \end{array} \right\} \text{millions of people}$$

   to travel freely in $\left\{ \begin{array}{l} \text{the computer would.} \\ \text{cyberspace.} \end{array} \right.$ 【正】

2. *Now he has become the symbol of the computer times.* 【誤】

   （景美女中 賴華沂同學）

   * 須將 computer times 改成 computer age（電腦時代）。

   → Now he has become the symbol of the

   computer $\left\{ \begin{array}{l} \text{age.} \\ \text{era.} \end{array} \right.$ 【正】

【註釋】 challenge〔'tʃælɪndʒ〕*n.* 挑戰
    allow〔ə'laʊ〕*v.* 讓
    run wild 不受拘束　achieve〔ə'tʃiv〕*v.* 達成
    be in *one's* **forties** 在某人四十幾歲的時候
    cyberspace〔'saɪbɚ͵spes〕*n.* 網路世界
    symbol〔'sɪmbḷ〕*n.* 象徵　age〔edʒ〕*n.* 時代
    era〔'ɪrə〕*n.* 時代

TEST 88

說明：下面一段短文中，有數處係以中文呈現，請利用上下
文線索（如單字、片語等）將其譯成正確、通順、達
意且前後連貫的英文。

Jerry was an amazing person who always looked on the bright side of life. When someone asked him how he was doing, he would reply, "If I were any better, I would be twins." When someone went to him complaining, 1. 他會向那人指出事情的光明面。 Even when once he was shot by an armed robber and was left lying on the floor, he didn't lose his optimism. What went through his mind was that he would finally have the chance to undergo an operation. 2. 他拒絕成為槍擊的受害者，並且存活下來。 From Jerry, I learned that one's attitude toward life makes a difference in the way he/she faces difficulties.

1. ....

2. ....

TEST 88 詳解

1. <u>*he would point at the bright side toward that person.*</u> 【誤】

* point at (指著) 須改為 point out (指出)，bright side 後面須加上 of things，且 toward 須改為 to。

→ he would point out to the person the

$$\begin{Bmatrix} \text{positive} \\ \text{good} \end{Bmatrix} \text{ side of things. 【正】}$$

2. <u>*He refused to be a victim of gun shot and survived.*</u> 【誤】

* gun shot 須改成 a gunshot (射擊)。

→ He refused to fall victim to the shooting
and survived. 【正】

【註釋】 amazing (əˈmezɪŋ) *adj.* 令人驚奇的
look on the bright side of ~ 看~的光明面
twins (twɪnz) *n. pl.* 雙胞胎
complain (kəmˈplen) *v.* 抱怨　　shoot (ʃut) *v.* 射擊
armed (ɑrmd) *adj.* 武裝的　　robber (ˈrɑbɚ) *n.* 強盜
leave (liv) *v.* 使處於 (某種狀態)
optimism (ˈɑptəˌmɪzəm) *n.* 樂觀
go through one's ***mind*** 掠過腦海
undergo (ˌʌndɚˈgo) *v.* 接受；經歷
operation (ˌɑpəˈreʃən) *n.* 手術
make a difference 有影響　　way (we) *n.* 方式
point out 指出　　positive (ˈpɑzətɪv) *adj.* 積極的；樂觀的
fall victim to 成為…的受害者　　survive (səˈvaɪv) *v.* 存活

TEST 89

Emily Dickinson was not the kind of person we expect to become a great poet. She was not an active person, stayed home all the time, and hardly ever saw anyone during her lifetime. She was a rather unusual person. However, she indeed wrote wonderful poems with deep meanings, 1.而且她現在被認爲是十九世紀最偉大的美國詩人之一。 In fact, Emily was good at using images from nature and everyday experience to express her ideas. In the poem *"I'm Nobody! Who Are You?"* we can see her unique observations of what it means to be human. 2.簡言之，想當大人物是要付出代價的。

1. ....

2. ....

TEST 89 詳解

1. *and she is now considered to be one of the greatest poets in the ninteenth century.*【誤】

   * greatest poets 須改為 greatest American poets，且 in the ninteenth century 須改為 of the nineteenth century。

   → and she is now $\begin{cases} \text{considered} \\ \text{regarded as} \end{cases}$ one of the

   $\begin{cases} \text{greatest American poets of the nineteenth century.} \\ \text{best nineteenth-century American poets.} \end{cases}$ 【正】

2. *In short, it needs to pay to be a somebody.*【誤】

   * it needs to pay to be a somebody. 應改成 there's a price for being (a) somebody.。

   → In short, $\begin{cases} \text{there's a price for being somebody.} \\ \text{being somebody has a price.} \end{cases}$ 【正】

【註釋】 poet (ˈpo‧ɪt) *n.* 詩人   active (ˈæktɪv) *adj.* 活躍的
   hardly ever 幾乎不曾   lifetime (ˈlaɪfˌtaɪm) *n.* 一生
   rather (ˈræðɚ) *adv.* 相當   indeed (ɪnˈdid) *adv.* 的確
   be good at 擅長   image (ˈɪmɪdʒ) *n.* 意象
   unique (juˈnik) *adj.* 獨特的
   observation (ˌɑbzɚˈveʃən) *n.* 觀察
   consider (kənˈsɪdɚ) *v.* 認為
   regard (rɪˈgɑrd) *v.* 認為
   in short 簡言之；總之   price (praɪs) *n.* 代價
   somebody (ˈsʌmˌbɑdɪ) *n.* 大人物；了不起的人

TEST 90

說明：下面一段短文中，有數處係以中文呈現，請利用上下文線索（如單字、片語等）將其譯成正確、通順、達意且前後連貫的英文。

New Thanksgiving traditions catering to people who lived in cities emerged. The day following Thanksgiving 1.漸漸就被大家知道是聖誕採購節的第一天。 Large companies began to sponsor lavish parades, which often drew millions of spectators. In this way, they could also attract many customers. As football became increasingly popular in the 1920s and 1930s, many people began to go to a football game as part of their holiday. Teams in the National Football League eventually established traditions of 2.在感恩節的下午進行全國電視轉播的比賽。

1. ....

2. ....

TEST 90 詳解

1. *gradually known as the first day of Christmas shopping days.*【誤】

   * known as 須改為 became known as，而 shopping days 須改為 shopping season (採購節)。

   $\rightarrow \left\{ \begin{array}{l} \text{gradually became} \\ \text{eventually came to be} \end{array} \right\}$ known as the $\left\{ \begin{array}{l} \text{first day} \\ \text{beginning} \end{array} \right\}$

   of the Christmas shopping season.【正】

2. *national TV broadcast's contest on Thanksgiving afternoon.*【誤】

   * 「進行」比賽須用 play，而「球賽」須用 games，「全國電視轉播的」是 nationally televised。

   → playing nationally televised games on Thanksgiving afternoon.【正】

【註釋】 Thanksgiving〔,θæŋks'gɪvɪŋ〕 n. 感恩節
    tradition〔trə'dɪʃən〕 n. 傳統
    cater to 迎合　emerge〔ɪ'mɝdʒ〕 v. 出現
    following〔'faləwɪŋ〕 prep. 在…之後
    sponsor〔'spɑnsɚ〕 v. 贊助　lavish〔'lævɪʃ〕 adj. 豐富的
    parade〔pə'red〕 n. 遊行　draw〔drɔ〕 v. 吸引
    spectator〔'spɛktetɚ〕 n. 觀眾
    increasingly〔ɪn'krisɪŋlɪ〕 adv. 越來越
    league〔lig〕 n. 聯盟　eventually〔ɪ'vɛntʃʊəlɪ〕 adv. 最後
    establish〔ə'stæblɪʃ〕 v. 建立
    season〔'sizn̩〕 n. 時期；時節　*shopping season* 採購節
    televised〔'tɛlə,vaɪzd〕 adj. 電視播送的

TEST 91

Little is known about Aesop. He seems to have lived and died in Greece some five hundred years before the birth of Christ. Aesop's fables always use animals to tell their stories. Sometimes the fables also have human characters. 1.無論寓言中的角色是動物或人，they have a weakness that gets them into trouble. Reading about their troubles, 2.我們獲得智慧並能洞察人性。

1. ....

2. ....

TEST 91 詳解

1. *No matter the role of fable is animal or human,*【誤】

（大直高中 林瑞怡同學）

＊須在 No matter 後面加上 whether，且 role of fable is animal or human 須改成 characters in a fable are animals or humans。

→ **Whether the characters in a fable are animals or humans,**【正】

2. *we can acquire wisdom and perceive humanity.*【誤】

＊perceive（察覺）須改成 understand。

→ we $\left\{\begin{array}{l} \text{gain} \\ \text{acquire} \end{array}\right\}$ wisdom and $\left\{\begin{array}{l} \text{insight into} \\ \text{an understanding of} \end{array}\right\}$

human nature.【正】

【註釋】 Aesop（ˈisəp）*n.* 伊索【為希臘「伊索寓言」(Aesop's Fables) 之作者】 some（sʌm）*adv.* 大約

Christ（kraɪst）*n.* 基督

before the birth of Christ 西元前（ = B.C. ）

fable（ˈfebḷ）*n.* 寓言 character（ˈkærɪktɚ）*n.* 人物

weakness（ˈwiknɪs）*n.* 弱點

acquire（əˈkwaɪr）*v.* 獲得

wisdom（ˈwɪzdəm）*n.* 智慧

humanity（hjuˈmænətɪ）*n.* 人性

insight（ˈɪnˌsaɪt）*n.* 見解；洞察力

human nature 人性

TEST 92

說明：下面一段短文中，有數處係以中文呈現，請利用上下文線索（如單字、片語等）將其譯成正確、通順、達意且前後連貫的英文。

In a survey conducted recently, 1.百分之六十的受訪者說他們相信外星人的存在 and around half of the college graduates surveyed said they believed that flying saucers had visited the Earth. Besides, more than half of the people polled thought that aliens were friendly rather than hostile. Since people around the world take a great interest in UFOs, many businessmen are therefore making money on this craze. 2.他們什麼都有賣，從填充的外星人玩偶到外星人冰箱磁鐵都有。

1. ....

2. ....

TEST 92 詳解

1. <u>*sixty percent of the interviewees said that they believe the*</u>
   <u>*existence of the alien*</u>【誤】（建國中學 陳政葦同學）

   * believe 須改成 believe in，且 the alien 須改成 aliens（外星人）。

   → 60 percent of the people asked said that they

   $\left\{\begin{array}{l}\text{believed in the existence of aliens}\\\text{were convinced that aliens exist}\end{array}\right.$ 【正】

2. <u>*They sell anything, from the stuffed alien doll to the alien*</u>
   <u>*fridge magnet.*</u>【誤】（建國中學 陳政葦同學）

   * anything 也可寫成 everything，而 doll 和 magnet 的字尾都須加 s。

   → They sell $\left\{\begin{array}{l}\text{everything}\\\text{all kinds of things,}\end{array}\right\}$ from

   stuffed alien dolls to alien refrigerator magnets.【正】

【註釋】 survey〔sə'veɪ〕*n. v.* 調查　conduct〔kən'dʌkt〕*v.* 進行；做
　　　　recently〔'risṇtlɪ〕*adv.* 最近
　　　　graduate〔'grædʒuɪt〕*n.* 畢業生
　　　　flying saucer 飛碟　　poll〔pol〕*v.* 做…的民意調查
　　　　alien〔'eljən〕*n.* 外星人　*adj.* 外星人的
　　　　rather than 而不是　　hostile〔'hastḷ, 'hastɪl〕*adj.* 敵對的
　　　　take an interest in 對…有興趣
　　　　UFO 幽浮；不明飛行物體（＝*unidentified flying object*）
　　　　craze〔krez〕*n.* 狂熱；熱中　　***believe in*** 相信有
　　　　existence〔ɪg'zɪstəns〕*n.* 存在
　　　　stuffed〔stʌft〕*adj.* 填充的　　fridge〔frɪdʒ〕*n.* 冰箱
　　　　magnet〔'mægnɪt〕*n.* 磁鐵

TEST 93

　　A shared language means easier communication and a foundation for trust. If people know a widely spoken language, 1. 他們不必害怕到很遠的地方去旅行。 Besides, their career options grow and their lives will certainly be enriched. However, it's a pity that the less common regional languages will soon disappear 2. 因為在現代世界中，將沒有它們的一席之地。

1. ....

2. ....

TEST 93 詳解

1. <u>*they don't have to be fear to take a trip far away.*</u> 【誤】

(師大附中 郭潤宗同學)

* be fear to take 須改成 be afraid to take 或 be afraid of taking。

→ they $\left\{\begin{array}{l}\text{need not fear traveling to}\\\text{don't have to be afraid of going to}\end{array}\right\}$

$\left\{\begin{array}{l}\text{distant}\\\text{faraway}\end{array}\right\}$ places. 【正】

2. <u>*because in the modern world, there will have no seats for*</u>
<u>*them.*</u> 【誤】 (師大附中 郭潤宗同學)

* 「there + be 動詞」表示「有」，故 have 須改爲 be。

→ because there will be no $\left\{\begin{array}{l}\text{place}\\\text{room}\end{array}\right\}$ for

them in the modern world. 【正】

【註釋】 shared (ʃɛrd) *adj.* 共有的
communication (kə,mjunə'keʃən) *n.* 溝通
foundation (faʊn'deʃən) *n.* 基礎
career (kə'rɪr) *n.* 職業；生涯　　option ('apʃən) *n.* 選擇
grow (gro) *v.* 增加　　enrich (ɪn'rɪtʃ) *v.* 使豐富
pity ('pɪtɪ) *n.* 可惜的事
regional ('ridʒənl̩) *adj.* 區域性的；地方性的
travel to 前往
faraway ('fɑrə'we) *adj.* 遙遠的 (= *distant*)
place (ples) *n.* 空間　　room (rum) *n.* 空間

TEST 94

> 説明：下面一段短文中，有數處係以中文呈現，請利用上下文線索（如單字、片語等）將其譯成正確、通順、達意且前後連貫的英文。

　　1.超級巨星會影響大眾的流行以及人們每天的穿著。

Increasingly, these celebrities are also using their fame to make a positive difference in the world. For example, Jackie Chan is well-known for helping Hong Kong's young people and being the Goodwill Ambassador. Another example is the famous talk show host Oprah Winfrey, 2.她運用自己明星的力量，來集中注意力到受苦的人身上。 Publicity follows famous people, no matter where they go or what they do.

1. ....

2. ....

TEST 94　詳解

1. *Super stars will effect the public fashion and people's dress.*【誤】

＊Super stars 應改成 Superstars，而 effect the public fashion 應改成 affect the popular fashion，且 dress 應改成 everyday dress（每天的穿著）。

→ Superstars $\begin{Bmatrix} \text{influence} \\ \text{have an effect on} \end{Bmatrix}$ popular fashions

and the way people dress every day.【正】

2. *she uses the star power to concentrates on suffer people.*【誤】

＊she 應改成 who，且 concentrates on suffer people 須改成 draw attention to suffering people。

→ who uses her star power to $\begin{Bmatrix} \text{focus attention on} \\ \text{draw attention to} \end{Bmatrix}$

those who are suffering.【正】

【註釋】 increasingly〔ɪnˈkrisɪŋlɪ〕*adv.* 逐漸地
celebrity〔səˈlɛbrətɪ〕*n.* 名人　　fame〔fem〕*n.* 名聲
make a difference 有影響；有差別
positive〔ˈpɑzətɪv〕*adj.* 正面的　***be well-known for*** 以…有名
Goodwill Ambassador 親善大使
talk show host 脫口秀節目主持人
publicity〔pʌbˈlɪsətɪ〕*n.* 受歡迎；出名
superstar〔ˈsupɚˌstar〕*n.* 超級巨星
influence〔ˈɪnfluəns〕*v.* 影響（= *affect* = *have an effect on*）
popular〔ˈpɑpjələ〕*adj.* 大眾的　fashion〔ˈfæʃən〕*n.* 流行
focus attention on 集中注意力於…　suffer〔ˈsʌfɚ〕*v.* 受苦

TEST 95

You may think that shyness isn't that widespread. But actually, shyness is a very common problem, much more common than we think. 1. 害羞的人總是覺得很緊張，而且他們會擔心給別人不好的印象。 Shyness doesn't necessarily show on the surface. Sometimes shy people are thought to be snobbish. In fact, they are afraid to make contact with people. They are often lonely and unhappy in social situations. From research, we know some shyness is innate, 2. 但是有些可能是因爲像離婚或失業這樣的危機造成的。 Whatever the reasons, shy people are ill at ease when teased, "Has the cat got your tongue?"

1. ....

2. ....

TEST 95 詳解

1. *Shy people always feel nervous, and they worry that they may make bad impression on other people.* 【誤】（建國中學 王劭予同學）

   * impression 爲可數名詞，故須改爲 bad impressions，或 a bad impression。

   → Shy people always feel nervous and they worry about

   { making a bad impression on people.
   { leaving people with a bad impression. 【正】

2. *but some may result in some crisis like divorce or unemployment.* 【誤】（建國中學 王劭予同學）

   * result in（導致）須改爲 result from（起因於）。

   → but some { may / might } be { caused by such crises / the result of a crisis }

   { as divorce / such as a divorce } or { job loss. / unemployment. } 【正】

【註釋】 shyness〔'ʃaɪnɪs〕 n. 害羞
widespread〔'waɪd'sprɛd〕 adj. 普遍的　　***not necessarily*** 未必
surface〔'sɜfɪs〕 n. 表面　　snobbish〔'snɑbɪʃ〕 adj. 勢利眼的
make contact with 和…接觸
social〔'soʃəl〕 adj. 社交的　　innate〔ɪ'net〕 adj. 天生的
ill at ease 心神不寧　　tease〔tiz〕 v. 嘲弄
Has the cat got your tongue? 貓咬住你的舌頭啦？；怎麼不說話？
nervous〔'nɜvəs〕 adj. 緊張的
impression〔ɪm'prɛʃən〕 n. 印象
some〔sʌm〕 adj. 某種；某些
crisis〔'kraɪsɪs〕 n. 危機【複數型爲 crises】
divorce〔də'vors〕 n. 離婚　　***job loss*** 失業（= *unemployment*）

TEST 96

The narrator of this story imagines that he is 17 years old and dead. He imagines how he drove his mother's car home from school and, 1. 因為他開太快，做了太多次瘋狂的冒險， he ended up in a terrible accident. He sees himself lying on the ground, his body bloody and mangled. He sees his mother and father identify his body. He sees his family and friends at his funeral. 2. 他大聲叫，要人把他叫醒，但是沒有人聽到他的聲音。 "Please don't bury me," he begs. He promises God that if he can have just one more chance, he'll be the most careful driver in the world. "All I want is one more chance," he says. "Please, God, I'm only 17."

1. ....

2. ....

TEST 96 詳解

1. *because driving too fast, making too many crazy adventures,*【誤】

（永平高中 彭紀堯同學）

　　* because 須改爲 because of，且 , making…adventures 須改爲 and taking…risks 或 and taking…chances。

　　→ because he was $\begin{Bmatrix} going \\ driving \end{Bmatrix}$ too fast

　　and taking too many crazy chances,【正】

2. *He shouted out loud, wanted someone to wake him up, but no one heard him.*【誤】（永平高中 彭紀堯同學）

　　* 依句意爲現在式，故 shouted 須改成 shouts；因兩動詞間無連接詞，故須將 wanted 改成 wanting；heard 須改成 hears。

　　→ He $\begin{Bmatrix} cries\ out \\ calls\ out \end{Bmatrix}$ for someone to wake him up,

　　but no one $\begin{Bmatrix} can\ hear \\ hears \end{Bmatrix}$ him.【正】

【註釋】　narrator〔'næretɚ〕*n.* 敘述者
　　　　　imagine〔ɪ'mædʒɪn〕*v.* 想像
　　　　　end up 最後　　bloody〔'blʌdɪ〕*adj.* 沾血的
　　　　　mangled〔'mæŋgld〕*adj.* 撕碎的；血肉模糊的
　　　　　identify〔aɪ'dɛntə,faɪ〕*v.* 辨認　　body〔'badɪ〕*n.* 屍體
　　　　　funeral〔'fjunərəl〕*n.* 葬禮　　bury〔'bɛrɪ〕*v.* 埋葬
　　　　　beg〔bɛg〕*v.* 乞求　　***take chances*** 冒險（= *take risks*）
　　　　　cry out for 大叫請求　　***wake sb. up*** 叫醒某人

TEST 97

> 說明：下面一段短文中，有數處係以中文呈現，請利用上下
> 文線索（如單字、片語等）將其譯成正確、通順、達
> 意且前後連貫的英文。

Young people, especially those who are at the age of 16, are most likely to stand in front of the mirror, examining every detail of their faces. They get annoyed 1.如果他們的鼻子太大，或有些青春痘快要冒出來。 The lovely boy or girl they like has not noticed them. Whatever they do, it seems that life is just never perfect. As for Alison, she never had such trouble because she was a beautiful, popular and smart student in the eleventh grade, not to mention an ocean lifeguard. 2.有著高挑苗條的身材、深藍色的眼睛，以及濃密的金髮， she looked more like a model than a high school student. She was always the focus of attention at every occasion.

1. ....

2. ....

TEST 97 詳解

1. *if their noses are too big or some pimples spring up.* 【誤】

(北一女中 林芳君同學)

* spring up 須改成 are springing up。

→ if their noses are too $\left\{ \begin{array}{l} \text{big} \\ \text{large} \end{array} \right\}$ or some pimples

are popping up. 【正】

2. *With slender body, blue eyes and hairy blond hair,* 【誤】

(北一女中 林芳君同學)

* body 為可數名詞，故須改為 a tall, slender body；blue 須改為
deep-blue，而 hairy (毛茸茸的) 須改為 thick (濃密的)。

→ With her tall, slim body, deep-blue eyes,
and thick blonde hair, 【正】

【註釋】 mirror (ˈmɪrɚ) *n.* 鏡子　　examine (ɪɡˈzæmɪn) *v.* 檢查
detail (ˈditel) *n.* 細節　　annoyed (əˈnɔɪd) *adj.* 惱怒的
lovely (ˈlʌvlɪ) *adj.* 可愛的　　smart (smart) *adj.* 聰明的
grade (ɡred) *n.* 年級　　***not to mention*** 更不用說
lifeguard (ˈlaɪfˌɡard) *n.* 救生員
more A ***than*** B　與其說是 B，不如說是 A
focus (ˈfokəs) *n.* 焦點　　attention (əˈtɛnʃən) *n.* 注意力
occasion (əˈkeʒən) *n.* 場合
pimple (ˈpɪmpl̩) *n.* 青春痘　　***pop up*** 冒出來 (= *spring up*)
slim (slɪm) *adj.* 苗條的 (= *slender*)
thick (θɪk) *adj.* 濃密的
blonde (bland) *adj.* 金髮的 (= *blond*)

TEST 98

説明：下面一段短文中，有數處係以中文呈現，請利用上下文線索（如單字、片語等）將其譯成正確、通順、達意且前後連貫的英文。

Generally speaking, geography and climate used to determine what people ate and how often they ate it. However, with the development of fast and convenient transportation, this is less true today. One of the factors is that 1. 科技的進步已經使得人們更容易取得來自全世界的食物。 In addition, as people continue to move from country to country, taking their foods and customs with them, they get familiar with the eating customs of different cultures. 2. 儘管如此，全世界大部分的地區仍然保有某種特定的飲食方式。 The reason for this still has something to do with geography. Take rice for example. Rice is easy to find and is commonly eaten in Asia, where rice is the major grain. On average, Chinese eat a pound of rice per person each day!

1. ....

2. ....

TEST 98 詳解

1. *the improvement of technique has already enabled people to get food from all over the world easier.*【誤】(中正高中 劉璇同學)

* 須將 technique (技術) 改為 technology (科技)，且句尾的 easier 須改為 more easily。

→ $\left.\begin{array}{l} \text{advances} \\ \text{improvements} \end{array}\right\}$ in technology have made it $\left\{\begin{array}{l} \text{easier} \\ \text{simpler} \end{array}\right\}$

for people to get foods from around the world.【正】

2. *Despite of it, most of the area in the world still remain some kind of eating habit.*【誤】(中正高中 劉璇同學)

* 須將 Despite of it 改為 Despite this，most of the area 須改為 most areas，而 remain (仍然) 須改為 retain (保留)，且 some kind 須改為 some particular kind。

→ $\left.\begin{array}{l} \text{Even so,} \\ \text{However,} \end{array}\right\}$ most $\left\{\begin{array}{l} \text{regions} \\ \text{areas} \end{array}\right\}$ of the world still

$\left\{\begin{array}{l} \text{keep} \\ \text{maintain} \end{array}\right\}$ certain particular eating styles.【正】

【註釋】 *generally speaking* 一般說來　geography〔dʒɪˈɑgrəfɪ〕*n.* 地理
used to 以前　determine〔dɪˈtɜmɪn〕*v.* 決定
transportation〔ˌtrænspɚˈteʃən〕*n.* 交通運輸
factor〔ˈfæktɚ〕*n.* 因素　*have something to do with* 和…有關
take～for example 以～為例　rice〔raɪs〕*n.* 稻米
commonly〔ˈkɑmənlɪ〕*adv.* 普遍地　Asia〔ˈeʃə〕*n.* 亞洲
major〔ˈmedʒɚ〕*adj.* 主要的　grain〔gren〕*n.* 穀物
on average 平均而言　advance〔ədˈvæns〕*n.* 進步
even so 儘管如此　region〔ˈridʒən〕*n.* 地區
certain〔ˈsɜtn̩〕*adj.* 某些　style〔staɪl〕*n.* 方式

TEST 99

Stress is not just caused by our mental or emotional condition. It is also influenced by whether we are physically exhausted, 1. 我們是否有均衡的飲食，以及我們是否知道如何放鬆。 Besides, whether or not something is stressful may change from day to day, even for the same person. In some situations, if we are rested and feel good about ourselves, a little stress will not be a problem. In others, if we are tired or feel unsure about abilities, 2. 即使是少量的壓力也可能會造成問題。

1. ....

2. ....

TEST 99 詳解

1. *whether we have a balanced diets, and whether we know how to relax.* 【誤】

    * 須將 a balanced diets 改成 balanced diets 或 a balanced diet。

    → whether we have a balanced diet and whether we know how to relax. 【正】

2. *even a little stress may cause problem.* 【誤】

    * problem 爲可數名詞，故須改爲 problems。

    → even a small amount of stress can

    $$\left\{ \begin{array}{l} \text{bring about} \\ \text{cause} \end{array} \right\} \text{problems.}$$ 【正】

【註釋】 stress〔strɛs〕*n.* 壓力（= *pressure*）
    cause〔kɔz〕*v.* 造成
    mental〔'mɛntḷ〕*adj.* 心理的
    emotional〔ɪ'moʃənḷ〕*adj.* 情緒的
    influence〔'ɪnfluəns〕*v.* 影響
    physically〔'fɪzɪkḷɪ〕*adv.* 身體上
    exhausted〔ɪg'zɔstɪd〕*adj.* 筋疲力盡的
    stressful〔'strɛsfəl〕*adj.* 有壓力的
    rested〔'rɛstɪd〕*adj.* 休息充足的
    balanced〔'bælənst〕*adj.* 均衡的
    diet〔'daɪət〕*n.* 飲食   ***bring about*** 導致；造成

TEST 100

The giant pandas today are facing extinction, and the biggest problem comes from the loss of their natural habitat. It's due mainly to deforestation. <u>1. 砍伐森林不只使得熊貓的棲息地消失，</u> but threatens the panda's food supply. In addition, without enough forest area, it is difficult for pandas to find appropriate mates. Besides, the young cubs of giant pandas are too vulnerable to grow up by themselves. They require a great deal of care from their parents. Luckily, measures are being taken by from the WWF and the Chinese government to help the pandas. The best way we can help the giant pandas <u>2. 就是要維護牠們的棲息地，並採取行動保護牠們的生命。</u>

1. ....

2. ....

TEST 100 詳解

1. *Deforestation not only makes the place of pandas to*
   disappear,【誤】（建國中學 劉承疆同學）

   * place 須改為 habitat（棲息地），且 makes 為使役動詞，故 to
     disappear 須改為 disappear。

   → Deforestation not only causes

   $$\left\{ \begin{array}{l} \text{panda habitats} \\ \text{the panda's habitat} \end{array} \right\} \text{to disappear,}$$ 【正】

2. *is to preserve their habitat, and take actions to protect their*
   lives.【誤】（建國中學 劉承疆同學）

   * take actions 須改為 take action（採取行動）。

   → is to $\left\{ \begin{array}{l} \text{preserve} \\ \text{protect} \end{array} \right\}$ their habitat

   and $\left\{ \begin{array}{l} \text{take action} \\ \text{do something} \end{array} \right\}$ to protect their lives. 【正】

【註釋】 giant〔'dʒaɪənt〕*adj.* 巨大的　　panda〔'pændə〕*n.* 熊貓
　　　　 extinction〔ɪk'stɪŋkʃən〕*n.* 絕種　habitat〔'hæbə,tæt〕*n.* 棲息地
　　　　 due to 由於　　mainly〔'menlɪ〕*adv.* 主要地
　　　　 deforestation〔dɪ,fɔrɪs'teʃən〕*n.* 砍伐森林
　　　　 threaten〔'θrɛtn̩〕*v.* 威脅　　supply〔sə'plaɪ〕*n.* 供給
　　　　 appropriate〔ə'proprɪɪt〕*adj.* 適當的
　　　　 mate〔met〕*n.* 夫或妻；對象　　cub〔kʌb〕*n.* 幼獸
　　　　 vulnerable〔'vʌlnərəbl̩〕*adj.* 易受傷害的
　　　　 require〔rɪ'kwaɪr〕*v.* 需要　　**a great deal of** 大量的
　　　　 care〔kɛr〕*n.* 照顧　　measure〔'mɛʒə〕*n.* 措施
　　　　 WWF 世界自然基金會（= *World Wide Fund for Nature*）
　　　　 not only…but (also)～ 不僅…而且～
　　　　 preserve〔prɪ'zɝv〕*v.* 保存；保護

心得筆記欄

劉毅英文「101年學科能力測驗」15級分名單

姓 名	學 校	班級	姓 名	學 校	班級	姓 名	學 校	班級
白善尹	建國中學	319	王文洲	建國中學	319	王欣維	台中一中	316
徐大鈞	建國中學	326	蔡睿庭	成功高中	314	李重甫	台中一中	320
張嘉仿	中崙高中	301	黃珮瑄	中山女中	3博	楊啓蘭	台中一中	324
施宇哲	建國中學	302	黃昭維	板橋高中	320	廖城武	台中一中	316
王奕婷	北一女中	3讓	黃懷萱	北一女中	3忠	沙志軒	台中一中	308
鄭育安	建國中學	319	陶俊成	成功高中	302	陳浩天	台中一中	314
吳萬泰	建國中學	323	陳羿愷	建國中學	312	李元裕	台中二中	314
陳琦翰	建國中學	329	曾昱豪	師大附中	1237	劉欣明	台中女中	318
詹士賢	建國中學	311	隋 毅	成功高中	305	吳芝宜	台中女中	309
張喬雅	延平高中	308	王薇之	中山女中	3群	陳慧齡	台中女中	312
陳昱達	建國中學	303	余欣珊	中正高中	306	賴好欣	台中女中	312
林述君	松山高中	319	李思嫻	市大同高中	304	徐毓禪	台中女中	314
李孟璇	景美女中	3平	戴晏寧	建國中學	321	陳綺婷	台中女中	310
廖子瑩	北一女中	3數	俞乙立	建國中學	319	姚凱瑜	台中女中	304
林耕熏	北一女中	3良	吳承恩	成功高中	322	李靖淳	台中女中	314
楊華偉	大同高中	313	蔡昀唐	建國中學	304	陳奕均	台中女中	304
薛羽彤	北一女中	3良	陳聖寶	中正高中	305	蔡孟涵	明道中學	308
吳冠廷	延平高中	310	關育姍	板橋高中	303	陳沐道	明道中學	304
龔柏儒	國立竹東	310	蔡宜潔	北一女中	3儉	徐子庭	長億高中	602
洪懿亨	建國中學	319	許維帆	建國中學	304	林晏如	國立大里高中	301
林芳寧	市大同高中	301	簡上祐	成淵高中	310	洪妮端	國立大里高中	304
高晟軒	成功高中	302	葉思芃	師大附中	1246	陳佳穎	國立大里高中	303
林上竣	建國中學	325	黃雅萱	北一女中	3御	王 嵐	華盛頓高中	301
黃莉晴	板橋高中	308	鄭之琳	中山女中	3忠	莊婷雅	曉明高中部	3乙
寇 軒	師大附中	1259	劉子銘	建國中學	329	詹宜穎	僑泰中學	307
陳俊達	板橋高中	317	林筱儒	中山女中	3群	王彥中	台南一中	319
吳昌蓉	延平高中	311	葉 蘋	板橋高中	305	林奕辰	台南一中	319
賴又華	北一女中	3毅	劉弘煒	師大附中	1257	汪廷翰	台南一中	319
林懿萍	中山女中	3業	樂 正	建國中學	325	王子誠	台南一中	317
陳仕軒	成功高中	321	何冠蓁	北一女中	3儉	林德軒	台南一中	302
李承芳	中山女中	3義	溫彥彰	建國中學	328	陳亮圻	台南一中	315
楊劭楷	建國中學	303	賴冠儒	永春高中	301	程冠連	台南一中	307
黃韻帆	板橋高中	320	廖唯翔	建國中學	328	涂昀朋	台南一中	307
李承翰	建國中學	325	蔡必婕	景美女中	3讓	郭品顯	台南一中	314
賈孟衡	建國中學	325	鄧鈺如	基隆女中	301	蔡昀知	台南一中	302
呂柔霏	松山高中	302	夏定安	北一女中	3毅	吳譽皇	台南一中	303
林柏鑫	延平高中	308	林裕騏	松山高中	310	蔡東哲	台南一中	312
吳柏萱	建國中學	307	鄭惟仁	建國中學	307	楊承煒	台南一中	301
鄭雅之	中山女中	3樂	望開怡	文華高中	302	周德峻	港明中學	3智
陳瑞邦	成功高中	313	王勻圻	文華高中	308	林姿伶	台南女中	310
魏宏旻	中和高中	311	陳映融	台中一中	310	林芝萱	台南女中	308
林育正	師大附中	1243	李淳懷	台中一中	302	林思妤	台南女中	312
高偉瀚	建國中學	313	游樑田	台中一中	319	陳廼婷	台南女中	311
陳信霖	建國中學	329	王勝輝	台中一中	324	黃涵纖	台南女中	319
陳俊霖	板橋高中	316	王奕閔	台中一中	318	陳琮翰	進 修 生	進修生
吳雨宸	北一女中	3俊	林宇勛	台中一中	317	黃偉綸	進 修 生	進修生
黃昱菱	市大同高中	313	羅笙維	台中一中	309	韓雅蓁	進 修 生	進修生
張軒羽	市大同高中	303	郭宇鈞	台中一中	317			

※ 尚未前來登記的同學，請回班登記。

劉毅英文家教班 101年指定科目考試榮譽榜

姓名	就讀學校	分數	姓名	就讀學校	分數	姓名	就讀學校	分數	姓名	就讀學校	分數
白善尹	建國中學	97	曾勝宏	海山高中	90.5	莊學鵬	松山高中	86.5	楊翔竣	台中一中	83
黃柏瑋	建國中學	97	陳亦韜	成功高中	90.5	劉嬉玹	中山女中	86.5	林嵩儒	內湖高中	82.5
林晏如	國大里高中	96.5	朱聖瀚	建國中學	90.5	王竣	板橋高中	86.5	鄭惟容	延平中學	82.5
姚又勤	建國中學	96	張景翔	師大附中	90	陳郁夫	師大附中	86	林子涵	松山高中	82.5
李思嫻	市立大同	95.5	吳姿萱	北一女中	90	呂柔霏	松山高中	86	徐瑀暄	師大附中	82.5
劉子銘	建國中學	95.5	李承芳	中山女中	90	陳翔緯	建國中學	86	曾怡安	景美女中	82.5
黃韻帆	板橋高中	95.5	黃禾軒	延平中學	90	廖寓宏	清水高中	86	張家華	成淵高中	82.5
張葳	松山高中	95.5	張任妏	台中一中	90	魏宏旻	中和高中	86	王于萱	新莊高中	82.5
楊啓蘭	台中一中	95	陳翔愷	建國中學	89.5	蔡宜潔	北一女中	86	黃安正	松山高中	82.5
陳綺婷	台中女中	95	李向元	景美女中	89.5	涂畇朋	台南一中	86	翟玉申	國大里高中	82.5
姚凱瑜	台中女中	95	張詩亭	北一女中	89.5	賴彥茹	台中一中	86	何佩璇	文華高中	82.5
林詠堂	建國中學	94.5	莊雅筑	國大里高中	89.5	張文馨	師大附中	85.5	李美嫻	文華高中	82.5
張容瑄	成功高中	94.5	楊凱丞	國大里高中	89.5	鄭之琳	中山女中	85.5	陳彥臣	建國中學	82
黃涵織	台南女中	94.5	吳昌晉	延平中學	89	陳思涵	板橋高中	85.5	陳俊承	泰山高中	82
張軒翊	市立大同	94	高婷柔	松山高中	89	李淳懷	台中一中	85.5	丁一瀚	中正高中	82
方智淵	建國中學	94	林晏佑	惠文高中	89	楊其臻	台中一中	85.5	鄧運鴻	成功高中	82
陶俊成	成功高中	94	楊劭楷	建國中學	88.5	楊華偉	大同高中	85	李昱翾	台南女中	82
葉書昂	台南一中	94	王繼鎏	內湖高中	88.5	辛安	中山女中	85	施侑杰	弘文高中	82
韓雅蓁	進修生	94	王鈞平	板橋高中	88.5	林耕熏	北一女中	85	陳艾筠	台中女中	82
蔡昱勻	內湖高中	93.5	張逸軒	建國中學	88.5	江易修	台南一中	85	謝兆糧	台中二中	82
葉蘋	板橋高中	93.5	賴冠儒	永春高中	88.5	施嵐昕	師大附中	84.5	李治緯	板橋高中	81.5
隋毅	成功高中	93.5	陳儀汶	內湖高中	88.5	陳建銘	延平高中	84.5	林俊瑋	建國中學	81.5
范祐豪	師大附中	93.5	胡婷勻	台南女中	88.5	詹欣蓉	海山高中	84.5	陳詩晴	復興高中	81.5
陳琮翰	進修生	93.5	陳佳穎	國大里高中	88.5	童褕	師大附中	84.5	阮顗瑄	成功高中	81.5
吳冠廷	延平中學	93	胡婷勻	台南女中	88.5	許博鈞	延平中學	84.5	黃宣堯	延平中學	81.5
李艾珊	岳高中	93	邱亦雯	板橋高中	88	林尚將	台南一中	84.5	周德峻	港明中學	81.5
許佑	成功高中	93	王立丞	成功高中	88	廖心妤	台中女中	84.5	陳偉翊	台南一中	81.5
張哲維	松山高中	92.5	林冠逸	中正高中	88	江柏融	格致高中	84	張巧慧	台中二中	81.5
鄭惟仁	建國中學	92.5	程冠連	台南一中	88	尤修鴻	松山高中	84	賴盈瑩	文華高中	81.5
吳雨宸	北一女中	92.5	吳譽皇	台南一中	88	廖唯朋	建國中學	84	周德峻	港明中學	81.5
羅笙維	台中一中	92.5	賴建中	國大里高中	88	張博翔	明道高中	84	林書宇	景美女中	81
王文洲	建國中學	92	程冠連	台南一中	88	黃懷萱	北一女中	83.5	廖郁心	衛道高中	81
鄭容安	建國中學	92	吳譽皇	台南一中	88	陳映睿	永平高中	83.5	林柏辰	台中二中	81
林立	建國中學	92	黃詣淳	中壢高中	87.5	趙仁豪	板橋高中	83.5	張碩穎	忠明高中	81
許維帆	建國中學	92	林展霆	建國中學	87.5	林鼎權	市立大同	83.5	林信宗	松山高中	80.5
黃珮瑄	中山女中	91.5	陳筱萱	崇光女中	87.5	蘇浩維	慈濟高中	83.5	張凱傑	建國中學	80.5
王薇之	中山女中	91.5	劉以增	板橋高中	87.5	張智婷	慈濟高中	83.5	闕君芮	內湖高中	80.5
黃詣霖	北一女中	91.5	陳建廷	彰化高中	87.5	蘇浩維	慈濟高中	83.5	雷力銘	東山高中	80.5
李冠頴	師大附中	91.5	翁子涵	麗山高中	87	徐瑞翊	建國中學	83	蕭芳祁	成功高中	80.5
徐季	北一女中	91.5	張凱翔	建國中學	87	林彥宜	內湖高中	83	游文瑜	內湖高中	80.5
黃柏榕	建國中學	91.5	曾鈺雯	中山女中	87	吳岱穎	內湖高中	83	簡上祐	成淵高中	80.5
汪廷翰	台南一中	91.5	陳柏犘	成功高中	87	林盈汝	中正高中	83	盧琮元	台南一中	80.5
鄭旭洋	台南一中	91.5	施宇哲	建國中學	87	鐘唯員	板橋高中	83	李雅筑	台南女中	80.5
施介紘	台中一中	91.5	歐亭妤	台南女中	87	白御宏	成功高中	83	王貫宇	台中一中	80.5
高偉瀚	建國中學	91	郭品臻	台南一中	87	陳信霖	建國中學	83	曾子柔	文華高中	80.5
張仕翰	建國中學	91	楊承燁	台南一中	87	張弘毅	泰山高中	83	陳亭甫	建國中學	80
劉宇軒	成功高中	91	林宇勛	台中一中	87	鄭雅之	中山女中	83	徐愷均	建國中學	80
蔡孟哲	建國中學	91	何廷橬	北一女中	86.5	鄧欣宜	板橋高中	83	葉思芃	師大附中	80
吳御甄	中山女中	91	莊庭秀	板橋高中	86.5	林盈舟	建國中學	83	廖宣懿	北一女中	80
林宜臻	台南女中	91	余欣珊	中正高中	86.5	溫彥彰	建國中學	83	鄧鈺如	基隆女中	80
陳筠暄	松山高中	90.5	陳子白	師大附中	86.5	龔子茵	師大附中	83			

劉毅英文家教班成績優異同學獎學金排行榜

姓名	學校	總金額	姓名	學校	總金額	姓名	學校	總金額	姓名	學校	總金額
蕭芳祁	成功高中	179250	李芳瑩	辭修高中	30550	郭清怡	師大附中	23700	柯姝廷	北一女中	19000
曾昱豪	師大附中	164500	李承芳	中山女中	30500	吳御甄	中山女中	23300	劉弘煒	師大附中	18900
賴宣佑	成淵高中	140250	賴佳駿	海山高中	30100	簡羿慈	大理高中	23000	李絃賢	板橋高中	18900
吳珞瑀	中崙高中	108800	吳思儀	延平高中	30100	張逸軒	建國中學	22700	劉湛	建國中學	18800
陳允禎	格致高中	108100	高行潯	西松高中	29700	蕭允惟	東山國中	22600	黃柏榕	建國中學	18700
林泳亨	薇閣國小	99000	丁哲沛	成功高中	29450	陳俊達	板橋高中	22600	林筱儒	中山女中	18600
陳亭甫	建國中學	94900	張薇貞	景美女中	29300	郭貞里	北一女中	22450	林裕騏	松山高中	18600
王千	中和高中	88300	邱逸雯	三重高中	29200	江品萱	海山高中	22300	賈孟衡	建國中學	18600
林渝軒	建國中學	88101	朱祐霆	成淵高中	29000	謝昀彤	建國中學	22167	位芷甄	北一女中	18450
蔡景勻	內湖高中	77000	賴佳瑜	松山高中	28300	吳承恩	成功高中	22000	林詩涵	南湖高中	18400
王資允	長春國小	66800	柯鈞崴	成淵高中	28200	王子豪	師大附中	21800	何思緯	內湖高中	18400
莊子瑩	薇閣高中	63600	吳書軒	成功高中	28000	吳萬泰	建國中學	21566	王志嘉	建國中學	18300
邱詩涵	市三民國中	59900	鄭惟仁	建國中學	27800	董澤元	再興高中	21500	蔡昀唐	建國中學	18200
薛羽彤	北一女中	59068	黃詩芸	自強國中	27500	陳琦翰	建國中學	21500	練冠霆	板橋高中	18100
羅姿涵	景美國中	57700	高昀婕	北一女中	27500	林瑋萱	中山女中	21500	黃筱雅	縣重慶國中	18000
蔡書旻	格致高中	54100	呂柔罪	松山高中	27450	戴嘉璨	建國中學	21375	何慧瑩	內湖高中	18000
徐大鈞	建國中學	53300	林俊瑋	建國中學	27400	劉家伶	育成高中	21300	李承翰	建國中學	18000
林臻	北一女中	51400	朱哲毅	師大附中	27400	陶俊成	成功高中	21100	戴秀娟	新店高中	17900
呂芝瑩	內湖高中	49750	何宇屏	陽明高中	27400	徐浩芸	萬芳高中	21100	廖珮琪	復興高中	17900
林立	建國中學	49075	劉奕廷	華江高中	27300	陳婕華	龍山國中	21000	李念恩	建國中學	17850
朱庭萱	北一女中	48817	黃堂榮	進修生	27100	張祐銘	延平高中	20950	林悅婷	北一女中	17800
陳瑞邦	成功高中	48300	蔡佳容	成淵國中	27050	賴冠儒	永春高中	20600	劉紹增	成功高中	17800
呂宗倫	南湖高中	47750	蔡佳恩	成功高中	27000	范祐豪	師大附中	20600	黃靖淳	師大附中	17750
林鈺恆	中和高中	46600	徐子洋	延平高中	26800	蕭允祈	東山高中	20550	林敬富	師大附中	17600
張立昀	北一女中	45367	邱奕軒	內湖高中	26750	袁好蓁	武陵高中	20450	林莛逸	中正高中	17600
林琬娟	北一女中	44483	許哲維	大直高中	26600	牟庭辰	大理高中	20400	林弘濰	師大附中	17550
賴鈺錡	明倫高中	42550	張景翔	師大附中	26600	吳姿萱	北一女中	20350	洪懿亨	建國中學	17500
陳彥同	建國中學	41266	李昕	育成高中	26200	林冠宇	松山高中	20350	王奕婷	北一女中	17500
鄭欣怡	政治大學	40500	王挺之	溪崑國中	26100	劉以增	板橋高中	20300	劉釋允	建國中學	17500
林清心	板橋高中	39500	陳昱勳	華江高中	26100	韓宗叡	大同高中	20200	林述君	松山高中	17450
黃珮瑄	中山女中	38850	陳明	建國中學	26050	俞乙立	建國中學	20100	楊舒涵	中山女中	17350
望皓宇	建國中學	38634	李威逸	松山高中	25900	趙于萱	中正高中	20100	林唯尹	北一女中	17300
鄭翔仁	師大附中	38450	楊舒閔	板橋高中	25800	吳元魁	建國中學	20100	黃詠期	建國中學	17100
羅偉恩	師大附中	38000	林懿萍	中山女中	25575	陳思涵	成功高中	20100	郭韋成	松山高中	17100
白善尹	建國中學	37800	練子海	海山高中	25500	盧安	成淵高中	20000	簡詳恩	桃園高中	17100
陳冠安	東海高中	37150	范照松	南山高中	25400	徐柏庭	延平高中	20000	蔡昕叡	松山高中	16900
楊玄詳	建國中學	36400	許晏魁	竹林高中	25350	張哲維	松山高中	20000	蔡承翰	成功高中	16900
謝家綺	新莊國中	35600	劉桐	北一女中	25300	楊于萱	新莊高中	20000	郭豪宴	市中正國中	16800
李祖荃	新莊國中	34000	梁耕瑋	師大附中	25100	羅之勵	延平國中部	19900	劉祖亨	成淵高中	16800
許瑞云	中山女中	33850	黃馨儀	育成高中	25100	曹騰羅	內湖高中	19600	蘇郁芬	中山女中	16800
陳冠勳	中正高中	33800	楊肇焙	建國高中	24900	卓晉宇	內湖高中	19600	周子芸	北一女中	16675
李佳翰	後埔國小	33000	吳雨宸	北一女中	24900	呂咏儒	建國高中	19500	鄭竣陽	中山女中	16650
歐庭安	金華國中	32800	黃安正	松山高中	24800	蔡必婕	景美女中	19400	周佑昱	建國中學	16400
趙啓鈞	松山高中	31950	簡上祐	成淵高中	24300	柯穎瑄	北一女中	19400	黃白雲	成功高中	16400
陳琳涵	永春高中	31650	魏宏旻	中和高中	24200	顏薇澤	華江高中	19400	許志遙	百齡高中	16400
黃韻帆	板橋高中	31400	劉子銘	建國中學	24200	賴又華	北一女中	19300	林政緯	成功高中	16300
蔡佳伶	麗山高中	31300	廖子瑩	北一女中	24166	廖宣懿	北一女中	19300	莊庭秀	板橋高中	16300
邵偉桓	大直高中	30950	龔毅	師大附中	24100	蔡柏晏	北一女中	19300	范文棋	中崙高中	16200
許顯升	內湖高中	30900	賴明煊	松山高中	23900	魏廷甜	陽明高中	19200	林仕衛	建國中學	16200
邱睿亭	師大附中	30850	陳羿愷	建國中學	23875	廖祥舜	永平高中	19100	方仕翰	南山高中	16100

姓名	學校	總金額	姓名	學校	總金額	姓名	學校	總金額	姓名	學校	總金額
洪敏珊	景美女中	16100	李姿穎	板橋高中	14200	方冠予	北一女中	12400	陳亦韜	成功高中	10800
趙家德	衛理女中	16100	鄭雅之	中山女中	14175	陳煒凱	成功高中	12400	林亭汝	景美女中	10800
許晉魁	政大附中	16050	詹士賢	建國中學	14100	陳亭儒	北一女中	12375	許令揚	板橋高中	10800
林俐妤	大直高中	16000	施嵐昕	師大附中	14100	盛博今	建國中學	12300	陳聖妮	中山女中	10700
林育正	師大附中	16000	鄭瑋伶	新莊高中	14000	蔣欣妤	板橋高中	12300	林芳寧	大同高中	10700
王思傑	建國中學	15900	呂胤慶	建國中學	14000	張好安	景美女中	12300	林筱芸	基隆高中	10700
鄭家宜	成淵高中	15900	劉裕心	中和高中	13950	陳怡卉	師大附中	12300	許馨文	新莊高中	10700
溫子漢	麗山高中	15850	陳映彤	中山女中	13900	陳昕	中山女中	12200	趙匀慈	新莊高中	10700
徐珮宜	板橋高中	15800	賴沛恩	建國中學	13900	江澐溱	復興商工	12200	陳赴妤	景美女中	10600
丘子軒	北一女中	15700	邱明慧	松山家商	13900	陳勁揚	大直高中	12200	林偉丞	林口高中	10600
郭昌叡	建國中學	15600	林書卉	薇閣高中	13800	謝松亨	建國中學	12200	葉宗穎	中正高中	10600
李姿瑩	板橋高中	15600	詹欣蓉	海山高中	13800	徐正豪	三興國小	12100	謝志芳	北一女中	10600
蔡濟伍	松山高中	15600	賴只晴	中山女中	13700	鍾宜儒	師大附中	12100	劉貞吟	永春高中	10500
廖婕妤	景美女中	15550	唐敬	松山高中	13700	趙祥安	新店高中	11900	趙昱翔	建國中學	10500
魯怡佳	北一女中	15533	施柏廷	板橋高中	13700	林宛儒	大直高中	11900	劉家宏	百齡高中	10500
蔡欣儒	碧華國中	15500	吳佩勳	松山高中	13600	廖珮安	祐德高中	11800	許晨健	新莊高中	10500
陳俐君	秀峰高中	15500	張詩亭	北一女中	13600	葉人瑜	建國中學	11800	陳耘慈	海山高中	10500
吳柏萱	建國中學	15500	黃乃婁	基隆女中	13600	范詔安	建國中學	11800	甯奕修	師大附中	10500
翁鈺達	格致高中	15500	李季紘	大直高中	13600	郭哲銘	西松高中	11800	秦嘉欣	華僑高中	10500
黃偉倫	成功高中	15500	饒哲宇	成功高中	13600	潘怡靜	成淵高中	11800	柯蒂任	大理高中	10500
陳胤竹	建國中學	15400	劉聖廷	松山高中	13575	邱彥博	華江高中	11700	林政瑋	板橋高中	10500
許佑	成功高中	15400	楊詠晴	三重高中	13400	陳冠廷	內湖高中	11700	陳品仔	師大附中	10450
張凱傑	建國中學	15300	王薇之	中山女中	13400	陳怡喧	中山女中	11700	陳書宇	景美女中	10400
童楷	師大附中	15300	林奐好	北一女中	13400	林憲宏	建國中學	11675	林詠堂	建國中學	10400
李孟璇	景美女中	15100	呂佳洋	成功高中	13400	劉秀慧	社會人士	11600	於祐生	成功高中	10400
王繼逢	內湖高中	15100	陳芝庭	麗山高中	13400	關育姍	板橋高中	11600	陳品辰	板橋高中	10400
郭權	建國中學	15000	陳仕軒	成功高中	13300	白宇玉	復興高中	11550	莊皓廷	建國中學	10400
林學典	格致高中	15000	薛宜軒	北一女中	13300	鄭博尹	師大附中	11500	王雯琦	政大附中	10300
蔡佳芸	和平高中	15000	曹傑	松山高中	13250	林崢	松山高中	11500	熊觀一	實踐國中	10300
王廷鎧	延平國中部	14900	黃玄皓	師大附中	13200	余思萱	松山高中	11500	呂佾蓁	南湖高中	10250
李冠頡	師大附中	14900	黃怡寶	西松高中	13200	莊學鵬	松山高中	11400	劉詩玟	北一女中	10200
黃姿瑋	中和高中	14800	王嘉紳	鷺江國中	13100	謝勝宏	建國中學	11400	陳韋翔	東山高中	10200
陳翔緯	建國中學	14800	張宛茹	基隆高中	13100	盧昱瑋	成淵高中	11350	傅鏡誼	永平高中	10200
顏士翔	政大附中	14800	潘羽薇	丹鳳高中	13100	陳彥鈞	泰北高中	11300	徐健文	松山高中	10200
張恩齊	成功高中	14700	雷力銘	東山高中	13100	陳毅	建國中學	11300	蔡欣翰	成功高中	10200
梁家豪	松山高中	14700	林承頤	延平高中	13100	劉傑生	建國中學	11300	蔡宗廷	師大附中	10200
尤修鴻	松山高中	14600	黃莉婷	板橋高中	13075	李盼盼	中山女中	11200	范詠晴	明倫高中	10200
陳品文	建國中學	14600	洪子晴	大同高中	12900	王立丞	成功高中	11200	洪千雅	育成高中	10200
鍾珮瑄	中崙高中	14600	牛筱苡	景美女中	12900	曾鈺雯	中山女中	11175	李品薔	林口高中	10100
張軒翊	大同高中	14500	簡笠庭	金山高中	12900	張雅婷	海山高中	11150	趙君傑	中和高中	10100
周大景	丹鳳高中	14500	葉慕神	樹林高中	12800	林昱寧	陽明高中	11100	許予帆	北一女中	10100
周東林	百齡高中	14400	高鈺珉	成功高中	12800	吳承叡	中崙高中	11100	林柏宏	師大附中	10100
林鼎翔	建國中學	14400	張仲豪	師大附中	12800	楊蕢琳	林口高中	11100	吳東緯	成功高中	10100
蔡佳妤	基隆女中	14400	葉玲瑜	北一女中	12700	劉懿萱	景文高中	11050	劉應傑	西松高中	10100
許丞鞍	師大附中	14300	吳冠廷	延平高中	12675	劉奕勖	師大附中	11000	施郁柔	中山女中	10100
卓漢庭	景美女中	14300	詹硯茹	石碇高中	12650	江瑞安	和平高中	11000	劉德謙	建國中學	10100
楊嘉祐	師大附中	14300	施衍廷	敦化國中	12600	胡予綸	成功高中	11000	陳怡蓁	新店高中	10000
張文馨	師大附中	14200	阮顯程	成功高中	12600	鄭維萱	百齡高中	11000	傅瀞萱	中山女中	10000
陳柏誠	松山高中	14200	吳重玖	建國中學	12575	粘書耀	師大附中	10900			
陳筠喧	松山高中	14200	許凱雯	北一女中	12500	鄭立昌	松山高中	10800			

※ 因版面有限，尚有領取高額獎學金同學，無法列出。

如何寫克漏式翻譯

主　　　編／劉　毅

發　行　所／學習出版有限公司　　☎ (02) 2704-5525

郵 撥 帳 號／0512727-2 學習出版社帳戶

登　記　證／局版台業 2179 號

印　刷　所／裕強彩色印刷有限公司

台 北 門 市／台北市許昌街 10 號 2 F　　☎ (02) 2331-4060

台灣總經銷／紅螞蟻圖書有限公司　　☎ (02) 2795-3656

美國總經銷／Evergreen Book Store　　☎ (818) 2813622

本公司網址　www.learnbook.com.tw

電 子 郵 件　learnbook@learnbook.com.tw

售價：新台幣一百八十元正

2012 年 11 月 1 日新修訂

ISBN 978-986-231-016-8